"Wh...
y...

"You know why, Renata." ...ice deepened to a seductive growl. ... you want me. Me, the man, not the prince. You want what I can give you, but not at the boutique or the jewelry store. You want what I can give you in the bedroom."

Oh, he had her there. The man wasn't even in the same borough with her and was making her crazy for him.

"Remember how I touched you last night?" She let out a moan in remembrance.

Undone by her own feminine nature. That one time had whetted her appetite for more. No question.

"That was just a taste of how it could be, Renata. Come with me." He paused, his deep breathing turning her on even more. "I command you."

Dear Reader,

Ever since I was a girl watching Princess Diana marry Prince Charles on live TV, I have been an avid royal wedding fan. My mother splurged on the miniature commemorative book and I spent hours poring over the photos with my sister. At one point, I had memorized the line of succession to the British throne!

Although the royal princes were a bit young for me, I still enjoyed reading about royal weddings—the beautiful brides, the (hopefully) handsome grooms, and most of all, the dresses. Satin, silk, velvet, taffeta. Diamond tiaras and pearls. When I thought of a trilogy surrounding three royal heroes and one royal wedding, I knew one heroine had to be a wedding dress designer.

Brash New Yorker Renata Pavoni designs hip, vintage-style gowns but definitely has a modern attitude—perfect to shake up the stuffy but sexy Prince Giorgio of Vinciguerra, accompanying his beloved sister Princess Stefania as she searches for the ideal wedding dress. Stefania selects the dress of her dreams, and Giorgio realizes he may have found the woman of his dreams.

A fun story about buying my own wedding dress—my mother and I met on her lunch hour, and it was the fourth dress I tried on. Once I put it on, I knew that was The Dress. Forty minutes of shopping might be a world record. Many years later, my good friend looked at my wedding portrait and told me, "That looks like Princess Diana's dress!"

Happy reading!

Marie Donovan

ROYALLY ROMANCED

BY
MARIE DONOVAN

First published in Great Britain 2013
by Mills & Boon, an imprint of Harlequin (UK) Limited,
Eton House, 18-24 Paradise Road, Richmond, Surrey TW9 1SR

© Marie Donovan 2011

ISBN: 978 0 263 90505 2

30-0313

Harlequin (UK) policy is to use papers that are natural, renewable and recyclable products and made from wood grown in sustainable forests. The logging and manufacturing processes conform to the legal environmental regulations of the country of origin.

Printed and bound in Spain
by Blackprint CPI, Barcelona

Marie Donovan is a Chicago-area native who got her fill of tragedies and unhappy endings by majoring in opera/vocal performance and Spanish literature. As an antidote to all that gloom, she read romance novels voraciously throughout college and graduate school.

Donovan worked for a large suburban public library for ten years as both a cataloguer and a bilingual Spanish story time presenter. She graduated magna cum laude with two bachelor's degrees from a Midwestern liberal arts university and speaks six languages. She enjoys reading, gardening and yoga.

Please visit the author's website at www.mariedonovan.com.

To Dad,
A prince in a book for a prince of a man in my book.
Happy reading!

1

"YOU'RE WHAT?" GIORGIO's gold pen dropped from his fingers and rolled forgotten off his polished wooden desk as he gripped his phone.

His sister, his *baby* sister, Stefania, giggled from four thousand miles away in New York City. "I'm engaged to be married." She repeated it in Italian to make sure he understood. *"Fidanzata."*

"But, but…" he stammered, normally not at a loss for words. "To whom? And when?"

"Well…" She drew out the news teasingly and then her excitement bubbled over in a rush. "His name is Dieter von Thalberg and we met a few months ago when he traveled here for business."

"Only a few months?" Giorgio interrupted. "And you want to marry him already?" Stefania was impulsive sometimes, but not foolish.

"Of course." She giggled again. "Oh, Giorgio, I can't wait for you to meet him." She lowered her voice. "He's German nobility from a little place in Bavaria. You have to trust me, I've never felt this way about any other man. When he kisses me and we…well, anyway…" He practically heard her blush as she continued the catalog of wonders that was Dieter.

Giorgio fought the urge to start an international incident over Dieter, his future brother-in-law, for showing her the wide world of womanly delights. Giorgio couldn't think of it in more specific terms without his fine lunch of sausages and polenta sitting uneasily in his stomach.

He sighed and wished he had finished the rest of the bottle of wine rather than restraining himself to the two glasses he normally imbibed.

Rotten Dieter.

He hoped the man's ancestral holdings were overrun with mold and rats. But then Stefania would be unhappy, and that was the last thing in the world Giorgio wanted.

Actually, he hoped Dieter had some money of his own for the ancestral holdings and wouldn't constantly hit Giorgio up for loans. Giorgio had enough trouble with his own palazzo, *molto grazie.*

"But, Giorgio, you must realize none of this will be official until you give us your blessing. Dieter insisted it be so."

Hmm. He quirked his mouth. It was true. As ruling head of the Most Serene Principality of Vinciguerra, Giorgio had the right to approve or deny betrothals of members of the royal family, i.e. his sister, Principessa Stefania Maria Cristina Angela Martelli di Leone. It said so on his business card. Well, not really.

The only other members of the royal family were his grandmother, who at eighty was not expected to seek permission to wed again, and himself: Giorgio Alphonso Giuseppe Franco Martelli di Leone, Prince of Vinciguerra. Long ago, Giorgio had decided that if he never wed and had the requisite heir-and-a-spare, he would pass the title to Stefania and her children. After all, he was an enlightened, twenty-first-century monarch. One with the power to send Dieter the Dunce packing. He snickered.

"Giorgio?" his sister asked nervously. "Are you still there?"

"Si, si." He lapsed into silence, pondering what to do and how many heavy items Stefania would hurl at his head if he refused her undoubtedly golden-haired, Teutonic Prince Charming.

"Come to New York," Stefania commanded.

"What? Now?"

"Yes, now. I called Grandma today and she told me to get you out of her hair. She says you're driving her nuts." Having spent most of her childhood in New York, Stefania had a definite command of American idioms.

"What?" Giorgio sat bolt upright in his ergonomic Corinthian leather chair. "I am doing no such thing!"

"She begs to differ. She says you poke your nose in on her day and night so she can't get any rest."

Now he was insulted. Their grandmother had had a nasty bout of flu that had settled into pneumonia. After a couple touch-and-go weeks of around-the-clock care, she had pulled through but still needed nursing visits, respiratory therapists, physical therapists and doctor visits. And it was his job to make sure they were doing their jobs. He was more at ease if he could be present for all their consultations.

He reconsidered. Maybe that was a bit too much. After all, his grandmother had run Vinciguerra while he was off at university and had absolutely no trouble making her wishes known. He could also have his assistant text him updates on her health.

"Yes or no, George!" his sister shouted. She only called him his American nickname when she was either very pleased with him or very annoyed. No bets on which it was this time.

"Fine, Steve!" he shouted in return, his matching temper surfacing. "I want to meet this German Romeo who thinks he's good enough for my only sister. If he's not up to snuff, forget it! You can finish your master's degree instead. I'm not paying university tuition to have you moon over some man you barely know."

"He is not *some* man! He is *my* man, and I know him very well."

Giorgio gritted his teeth at her implication and forced himself to take several deep breaths. If he pressed his sister too hard, she was likely to elope to Vegas with the guy. "If you think so highly of him, Stefania, I will be happy to meet him."

"Fine." She sounded mollified, for the moment at least. With Stefania, you never could tell. "And I *am* finishing my degree, you know. If I take an extra course each semester, I'll be able to graduate next spring."

"That's wonderful news." He checked his schedule on his phone. "I can fly into New York Wednesday if that would work for you. And Dieter," he added grudgingly.

"Great! We'll meet for dinner Thursday, just the three of us."

"Great," he parroted, with much less enthusiasm. "I look forward to it."

"No, you don't, but thanks for saying so."

"Insincerity has its place, Steve. I would appreciate a tiny bit more insincere flattery from you, for example. 'Oh, my princely brother, if it pleases you to meet the unworthy specimen who has asked for my dainty royal hand in marriage…'"

She snorted. "If you wanted me to be dainty and insincere, you should have left me in Vinciguerra after Mama and Papa passed away."

"You know I couldn't do that, *piccina mia*." *My little one*—it was what their papa had called her, at least when she wasn't raising hell. Some things never changed.

"I know, Giorgio, and I love you for it."

He cleared his throat, which was developing a sudden lump. "I love you, too," he muttered. Words of love never came easily for him, even for his beloved sister.

"*Ciao*, Giorgio." She made a kissing noise into the phone and hung up.

He spun his chair to stare at the terraced vineyards beyond his office, the land still leafy and green in the April sun after a wet spring.

Springtime and young love. Giorgio's lips pulled into a wry smile. He remembered how romantic New York City could be in the spring. Unlike Stefania's Dieter, though, he had never been tempted to propose to anyone. He'd been busy with his education and bracing himself to return to Vinciguerra.

And now he would return to New York. It had been so long since he had been a foolish young student in the city. He straightened in his chair, the idea sounding better by the minute. He hadn't even had a free day in what seemed like forever, his every action in Vinciguerra witnessed and gossiped over by his loyal subjects. And to date any of them? Unthinkable.

He grimaced and tried to roll the kinks out of his neck. It wasn't as if he had any free time to date anyone, Vinciguerran or not. He pressed the intercom to call his assistant. "Alessandro? Please make arrangements for me to join Princess Stefania in New York tomorrow." He rubbed the back of his neck. Stefania would give him grief if she thought he looked scruffy for her big dinner.

"Oh, and also make an appointment with my barber."
Women always loved a fresh haircut.

"Renata?" Renata Pavoni's assistant, Barbara Affini, who
was also her aunt, stuck her perfectly coiffed, poufy head
of black hair into Renata's workroom.

"Hmm?" she mumbled around a mouthful of straight
pins as she pinned the white satin hem of a wedding dress.
The dress dummy stood on a carpeted platform, high
enough that Renata didn't have to crouch to work with the
fabric.

Barbara tsked and came into the room. "Your mama
would have a fit if she saw you like that. If you swallow a
pin, I'm going to call your brother's firehouse to take you
to the hospital and you'll never hear the end of it."

Renata spit out the pins and stuck them into a tomato-
shaped pincushion. "Okay, okay. Hey, how does this look?"

"Short."

Renata sighed. Why did she bother asking? It was the
same answer every time. "It's supposed to be short, Aunt
Barbara. It's a vintage-style wedding dress." Nineteen-
fifties and -sixties fashions were hot as hell, thanks to several hit TV shows and movies set in those time periods.

"Your cousins' wedding dresses, now those were clas-
sics," her aunt reminisced.

Renata pulled a face, glad her aunt was behind her. Her
petite cousins had rolled down the aisle in dresses wider
than they were tall, looking like those plastic doll head and
torsos on top of crocheted toilet paper holders. Thank God
wedding dresses from the eighties were still out of fashion.
She'd go broke buying miles of satin and tulle and pounds
of sequins.

Why had she hired her aunt? Oh, yeah, her uncle Sal
had begged Renata to get his wife out of the house. She

needed someone to mother once their youngest married, and the newly retired Sal wasn't about to volunteer for the vacancy.

Plus, Barbara was a fantastic seamstress and put the *p* in punctual.

Renata finished pinning the hem and stood, her knees popping. "The bride is coming in for her final fitting tomorrow. Will you have time to hem this?"

Her aunt sniffed. "Child's play. I even have time to add some sequins on the skirt if you'd like?" she asked hopefully.

Renata shook her head. "No sequins." Her client was an avowed hipster and would bite the sequins off with her teeth before wearing them down the aisle.

"Seed pearls?"

"Nope."

"How about some white-on-white satin-stitch embroidery?" But her aunt knew when she was beaten, her plump shoulders already slumping.

"Sorry." Renata *was* sorry. Her aunt would like nothing better than to hand-bead, hand-sequin and hand-embroider a gigantic ball gown with a twenty-foot train. But customers for gowns like that didn't come to Renata's design studio, Peacock Wedding Designs.

Instead, the dress in front of them was pretty typical of her sales—a fifties-style vintage reproduction with gathered halter straps and a full-circle skirt complete with a tulle crinoline. The bride was planning on a short, wavy fifties 'do and a small satin hat with a tiny net veil to drape over one carefully made-up eye.

Renata smoothed the skirt and carried it into the alteration workshop for her aunt. She caught a glimpse of herself in the three-way mirror and sighed. She loved vintage clothing but it sometimes didn't stand up to the modern workday. Her ivory linen blouse was wrinkled and her navy pencil skirt had twisted around her waist so the back slit was somewhere along the front of her thigh. She patted her auburn hair back into its nineteen-forties-style roll.

Her aunt noticed her self-grooming and finally smiled. "You look just like old photos of my dear mamma, God rest her soul."

"Thanks, Auntie." She blew her a kiss and fixed her skirt. She probably needed to touch up her lipstick, too. While lush red lips were historically correct, they did require more maintenance and she had to be careful that she didn't trip over her feet and plant a big red smacker on her pure white fabric. The things one did for fashion. Or at least her grandmother's fashion.

Renata hopped onto the elevated chair at her design table. Before she could uncap her cherry-red tube, the phone rang. "Peacock Wedding Designs, this is Renata."

"Hi, I've been looking at your website and I was wondering when I could come in to look at your dresses." The New York voice was young but confident, typical of her clientele. Brides who wanted a vintage look were not shrinking violets.

Renata flipped through the appointment calendar. "We can see you Friday."

"Are you free tomorrow afternoon?"

Renata wrinkled her nose. She'd been planning to take the afternoon off for the opening of a new art exhibit at a gallery in Manhattan. Her friend Flick knew a couple of the artists.

Her potential client hurried on. "I want my brother to come with me, and he's flying into town tonight."

Business was business, and maybe Brother was paying for the dress. "No, that's fine. What time is good?"

"Noon?"

"Great." Maybe she could see the opening after all—it started at two. "And your name?"

"Stefania di Leone." She had a perfect Italian accent when she pronounced her name.

"Ah, Stephanie of the Lion." Renata laughed. "My full name is Renata Isabella Pavoni—peacock. That's where I got the name for my salon."

"I think your designs are wonderful," Stefania enthused. "I looked in the bridal mags, but everything there is too over-the-top. I don't want a gigantic, poufy dress, or a corset-slip that looks like I forgot to put the rest of my dress on. And don't get me started on the mermaid style. I want to be able to *dance* at my wedding." She ended in a plaintive note.

Renata penciled her name into the calendar. "I'm sure you can find something you love. Have another look at my website and jot down some styles you'd like to try on." She gave Stefania directions to her salon in Brooklyn. Renata wished she could afford space in Manhattan, but even marginal neighborhoods there were exorbitant.

But Stefania didn't seem fazed. "My brother and I will see you tomorrow. Oh, I'm so excited! My first time wedding dress shopping!"

That could be good or bad, depending on if she made up her mind quickly or liked to browse. Either way, it was an opportunity. They said their goodbyes, and Renata hung up.

Barbara appeared in the doorway again. "Who was that, dear?"

"A bride is coming in tomorrow at noon to look at the dresses."

Her aunt made a disappointed face, her penciled eyebrows drooping. Since Renata had planned to take the afternoon off, her aunt made an appointment for Uncle Sal's annual colonoscopy. Lucky Sal.

"I'll be sure to keep you posted. And who knows? She may want a little more embellishment on her dress."

Barbara brightened. "That would be wonderful! I have lots of ideas."

"Great. Write them down. Or draw them."

She made a dismissive gesture. "Renata, you know I can't draw worth a lick."

"Ask your granddaughter Teresa to draw it for you. Isn't she a good artist?"

"Oh, well…" Her aunt fluttered her fingers at her bosom. "I'll have to see…my ideas probably aren't very good."

"You won't know until you try." Her aunt was a product of her times, discouraged from attending college and encouraged to marry straight out of high school. It was about time her aunt focused on herself instead of her family. Her family would be grateful, too.

"But I *can* hem that dress. I know I'm good at that."

"You are indeed." Renata gave her an encouraging smile and checked on the selection of samples she had in stock. Kick-ass. Her new bride would love them.

Unlike her aunt, she didn't have any doubts about her abilities. Renata loved vintage clothing, but she sure didn't have a vintage attitude.

2

"OUR LITTLE STEVIE's getting married?" Giorgio's old friend Francisco Duarte das Aguas Santas was obviously as dumb-founded as he had been. Once Giorgio's call from the VIP lounge in Leonardo da Vinci Airport in Rome had reached Frank at his ranch in the Portuguese countryside, it had taken several minutes to explain the situation.

"Yes, she's engaged." It was getting somewhat easier to say the words aloud. Giorgio's grandmother had been ec-static at the prospect of a royal wedding in Vinciguerra, especially since his own parents' wedding had been the last one celebrated, and that had been over thirty years ago. They had been returning from an anniversary trip when they died tragically in a car accident. Giorgio hoped his sister's nuptials would distract his grandmother from asking him when he would make some lucky woman his *principessa*.

"And to some guy we've never met." Frank sounded nearly as disgruntled as Giorgio had been.

"I'm leaving in a few minutes for New York, so I'll meet him tomorrow."

"Does Jack know?" Jacques de Brissard was the third member of their trio.

The three men had met their freshman year at the university in Manhattan. Although Giorgio technically outranked Frank, a duke with a large estate in Portugal, as well as Jack, a count who owned a lavender farm in Provence, they had much in common. Their bachelor apartment had turned into a home when Stefania had come to live with them—home, something Giorgio thought he'd lost when his parents died.

"No, I left a message for him, but he's traveling to Southeast Asia to do medical relief for that cyclone that hit the coast."

Frank made a sound of dismay. "He just got back from the earthquake in Turkey and sounded exhausted. I told him he needed to take some time off to recuperate. What is he thinking?"

"He's a doctor, and his patients come first." Giorgio didn't like it any better than Frank, but Jacques had always been single-minded about his medical career.

"He's going to wear himself out," Frank predicted gloomily, breaking off to shout instructions in Portuguese. Giorgio must have caught him as he was supervising the farmhands. Frank was always experimenting with new crops in addition to the olives and grapes his family's land produced. "But what are we to do with Stefania? She's not old enough to marry."

Giorgio shook his head to decline a second glass of wine from the lounge attendant, a pretty redhead. "I don't like it, either, Frank, but she's twenty-four. At least she's finishing up her graduate degree first. Besides, if you think she was stubborn when she was eleven…"

Frank snorted. "Remember when she refused to go to that fancy prep school you had all picked out for her and insisted on going to the academy of the arts? You even threatened her as her principality's sovereign ruler and what did she do?"

"Called the State Department and requested legal asylum on grounds of persecution." Giorgio sighed. He had tried to forget that little incident. His grandmother had not been amused to receive indignant phone calls from various human rights and refugee organizations.

"*Amigo meu,* maybe it *is* time to turn our girl over to this German fellow. After all, they are the orderly sort." He laughed, and Giorgio had to join in at the idea of anyone keeping Stefania in order. "And when is the blessed event? If she wants to come to my island out in the Azores she and the German can have a private honeymoon—consider it my gift."

Giorgio smiled. "They haven't set a date, but I'll be sure to tell Stefania when I see her Wednesday."

"Give her my love, and make sure this fiancé of hers is a decent guy. If he isn't, then you and Jack and I will talk some sense into her."

"Or I'll just drag her back to Vinciguerra and put her in the dungeon." They had three actually, one cleaned up for the tourists and two that hadn't been used since the Napoleonic Wars.

"Human rights organizations be damned." Frank sounded more cheerful. "We're just living up to the time-honored European tradition of locking stubborn princesses in towers and such."

"Do the time-honored traditions mention princesses with black belts in tae kwon do cleaning their brother's clock?"

"You can only blame yourself for that. You insisted she go to those self-defense classes if she was going to travel to the arts school in that awful neighborhood." Frank laughed. "Come on, things will be fine. If her young man is okay, then pick a date. Jack and I will help you plan her wedding—don't worry."

"The three of us?" Giorgio yelped. "Since when are we wedding experts?" He had fought very hard to be the exact opposite.

"Once you get the dress and the date, everything else falls into place. My mother planned my sisters' weddings. We run large estates—hell, you even run a whole country. How hard could it be?"

"You weren't even living in Portugal at the time—you merely flew in for the weddings and missed months of preparation."

"I did see some of what my mother and her wedding planners did." Frank sounded a bit hurt. "They have notebooks at the bookstore that explain what to do."

"Fine, okay, Frank, we'll all help Stefania as much as we can." Giorgio had no intention of being the lead wedding planner. It sounded like a nightmare in the making.

"*Maravilhosa.* Great." Frank cheered up. "I'll fix up the island however she likes. And I'm good for several barrels of the family sherry."

Giorgio could use a barrel of sherry about now, but his flight was about to board. "Thanks again, Frank. I'll keep you posted."

"Send me the report on her fiancé from the private investigator when it comes in. *Adeus!*" His friend hung up.

Giorgio wasn't sure if Frank was kidding or not about having Dieter investigated. Probably *not* kidding. He tapped his fingers on the small glass table. Should he? Stefania had several million euros in trust funds, some of which were to be released on either her marriage or her twenty-fifth birthday, both coming up within the next year.

He sighed, remembering the trouble some other European royals had run into with their unwise marriages.

Maybe erring on the side of caution…he quickly called his assistant. "Alessandro? Please call that private investigator from that insurance fraud case last year and have him research my sister's fiancé."

Oh, well. If Stefania found out and lost her temper with him, it wouldn't be the first time—or the last.

"WELCOME TO PEACOCK DESIGNS—you must be Stefania." Renata came from behind her workstation and warmly shook the bride's hand. She would be a dream to dress, slim but not too skinny, with rich brown eyes and olive skin. Her dark hair lay in curls on her shoulders. She looked like she should be modeling for an Italian tourism poster.

"Yes, I'm Stefania di Leone." Her bride gazed raptly around the salon. "The dresses are all so wonderful. I can't wait to get started." She made a beeline for a full-skirted, tea-length dress.

"Would you like to try this one?" May as well jump right in.

"Absolutely!" She pointed at the other dresses. "And that one, and that one, and that one."

Renata took her client's expensive leather coat and hung it next to her. "The changing room is right here." She ushered Stefania across the pearl-gray carpet into the large curtained alcove that served as her changing room and hung a couple of dresses on the hooks.

Stefania pulled off her pine-green sweater and then stopped. "George! I almost forgot."

"George?"

"My brother—he got a phone call right before we arrived here so he dropped me off. He should be here by now." She pulled an expensive phone out of her leather purse and rapidly sent a text. "There. I told him to get off the phone and get his butt in here."

Renata tried to hide a grin. Good luck with trying to get a guy off his phone and into a bridal salon.

"Do you mind sticking your head out to see if he's here?" Stefania unbuckled her belt. "George is definitely out of his element in a place like this."

"Aren't they all?" Renata backed out of the alcove and made sure the curtains were closed before she went looking for the missing George di Leone. Poor guy. She had conjured up a picture of the hapless Italian brother of the bride, nice enough but not a clue about fashion—just like her own brothers. Probably about average height, maybe running a bit thick around the middle from too much of Mamma's lasagna and cannoli—like her own brothers.

And then *he* walked in.

Renata forced herself to close her jaw at the specimen of exotic Italian manhood that had stepped into her humble little shop.

Not like her brothers, thank the good Lord. A couple inches over six feet, black wavy hair and emerald-green eyes set against the same olive skin as Stefania and no lasagna potbelly in sight. His hair was perfectly cut, short over the ears and slightly longer on top.

He was dressed like Cary Grant in a fantastic suit tailored in Italian charcoal wool by a master. Renata couldn't even begin to guess how much that would have set him back, combined with the finely woven snow-white shirt and expensive gold silk tie.

Renata smoothed her hands along her hips, fiercely glad she'd worn her high-waisted, ruby red 1950s "wiggle" skirt and snug-fitting black blouse. "Are you George?"

"George?" His honeyed voice positively dripped sex, even with that one syllable. "Ah, yes. Stefania has wasted no time. She calls me George." He spoke perfect English with a charming Italian accent.

"I'm guessing you're actually Giorgio." Giorgio di Leone—the lion. Rrrrrawww. She'd purr for him anytime.

"You may call me whatever you'd like, *signorina*. And what may I call you?"

"Renata Pavoni. This is my shop." She offered her hand and he took it, bowing slightly in a European manner.

He released her hand slowly and looked around the shop. "And these are the bridesmaid dresses?" He gestured at a short strapless number in blush pink satin and tulle.

"It could be—but that's a popular style for many brides, as well."

He stared harder. "That is a wedding dress? And so is this?" One had black leaves embroidered on the white satin skirt with a black-trimmed chiffon petticoat.

"Those are perfect for an informal wedding, not necessarily a church wedding. For example, one bride who sang in a rock band got married onstage in a gown much like this to her lead guitar player. They gave a concert after the ceremony."

"A rock band wedding?"

"Lots of fun," she reassured him. She had attended that wedding and had enjoyed the trip down memory lane when they played several hits from her Goth-girl phase. "But not for everyone." She wouldn't tell him about the tiny embroidered black skulls the rocker bride had requested for one of her petticoats. Aunt Barbara had flatly refused to do that embroidery—the handwork of the Devil, she called it, so Renata had sewn skulls until she saw reverse images of them when she closed her eyes at night. Not exactly sweet dreams.

"Not for Stefania. She is having a church wedding." That was Big Brother putting his foot down. Renata hoped that was Stefania's plan, as well. She had a feeling brother and sister were evenly matched in the stubbornness department.

"Many of the dresses are quite appropriate for a church wedding, if that is what Stefania has in mind. Excuse me, I need to check on your sister." She'd been so wrapped up in the brother that she'd almost forgotten about the bride. And if the bride wasn't happy, nobody was happy.

Renata poked her head through the cubicle curtain. Stefania sat on the gray velvet chaise texting someone. She'd been interrupted while undressing and wore a lacy bra and jeans. She looked up from her phone. "Sorry. Dieter is flying home from England and wanted to text me before they make him turn his phone off."

"No problem—let me know when you're ready." Renata wasn't exactly unhappy to return to Giorgio. He still stood politely, waiting for her. She'd forgotten that some men still had old-fashioned manners and would not sit down while a lady was standing. She gestured to the white leather—okay, it was vinyl—couch. "Please, Giorgio, have a seat. Your sister is texting her fiancé before his plane takes off."

"Only if you sit with me for a minute."

Renata hesitated. She never sat down during an appointment, was usually too busy to do so. And she never, ever sat with the bride's family, even if it only consisted of an extremely sexy older brother. She was there to work, not flirt.

"Please, *signorina*. I will not sit unless you do. My grandmother taught me better manners than that, and what kind of man would I be to embarrass my grandmother?"

Okay, now he was flirting, but subtly, not in a wolf-whistle, kiss-the-tips-of-his-fingers type flirting. Maybe she'd flirt back, if she wasn't too rusty to remember how. "If you insist, but only until Stefania needs me."

"Of course." He waited for her to settle onto the couch before sitting about eight inches away from her.

Renata rested her hands on her knees, acutely aware

of his presence. He was the epitome of men's elegance, his silk-clad ankle resting on the opposite knee, his black leather shoes immaculately polished. Even his cologne was classy and masculine, the scent of star anise and sandalwood rising off his warm caramel skin. Her nipples tightened under her blouse and she shifted on the couch to distract herself—in vain, of course. Well, she was a warm-blooded American woman with the male equivalent of an all-you-can-eat Italian buffet sitting next to her, complete with dessert. Mmm, Giorgio as dessert…she thought about that until she realized his delicious lips were speaking.

"Stefania is quite the whirlwind. She did not give you any information about herself or the wedding?" For some reason, he leaned forward, almost as if to gauge her reaction.

Back to business. "None at all. She told me over the phone that she'd just become engaged and was bringing her brother to shop for a wedding dress. I assumed the rest of your family was back in Italy and couldn't come over right away."

He sat back and sighed. "The rest of our family is our grandmother, who is indeed back in Italy, recovering from pneumonia."

If his grandmother was all he and Stefania had left…oh, dear.

He must have read her growing dismay. "Yes, unfortunately, our parents were killed in a car accident many, many years ago." He shrugged wide shoulders. "*Nonna* and I raised Stefania as best as we could, but searching for a wedding dress to wear on what I hope will be the happiest day of my sister's life?" He clenched his hands on his knees. "This is for our mother to do, not a stupid older brother."

Renata grabbed his hand, wrapping her fingers around his tense ones. "You are not stupid. Stefania waited to come in because she wanted you here with her. I know you both must miss your mother, but you are the person she loves and needs for this."

He looked down at their entwined fingers. She inwardly groaned. Her impulsive nature had gotten the best of her again and now she was holding hands with her client's sexy brother whom she'd met, oh, approximately twelve minutes ago. Talk about professional and businesslike.

She tried to tug her hand away, but he tightened his grip. "Signorina Renata, how did such a beautiful, young lady become so wise?"

An unladylike snort escaped her. "Years of foolishness."

The curtain rustled. "Renata, how do you zip this?" Stefania called.

Renata leaped to her feet as if one of her straight pins had fallen into the cushion and stabbed her in the butt. "Excuse me, please." He was there for dress-shopping, not getting mushy glances from the hired help. Giorgio released her hand and stood politely as she disappeared into the dressing room.

The bride held the bodice against her and Renata zipped up the back, slipping into sales mode. "All right, this is a tea-length, white lace dress over a white tulle petticoat. As you can see, the skirt is very full." So full that it was pushing Renata away from the bride as she fastened the hook-and-eye closure at the top of the zipper. "It has three-quarter-length sleeves that reach about to the middle of your forearm and a wide neckline that shows off your neck and shoulders nicely." She backed away so Stefania could get the full picture of how she would look.

"Is it the lighting or is there some pink at the bottom?"

"Yes, the neckline and petticoat are hemmed with a pale pink thread for decoration."

Stefania shook her head. "Not for me."

"No problem." Renata helped her out of the dress and carefully hung it up. "Here's one without the pink." Renata fitted her into a few more white dresses but Stefania just looked at herself in the mirror with a worried look.

"Sorry, Renata. I'm not usually this picky."

"Yes, you are," her brother called over the curtain.

"Can it, George," she retorted. "This is important."

Renata intervened. "You want to make sure to get the right dress for your special day."

"Whatever you pick will be a trend-setter," Giorgio predicted. What a nice brother—her own brothers would be loudly pitying whatever poor idiot Renata had suckered into marrying her.

"Yeah, I know." Stefania still looked glum. And pale, which was odd considering her beautiful warm skin tone.

"How often do you wear white?" she asked.

Stefania twirled back and forth, her eyes glued to the mirror. "I have a nice winter-white cashmere coat, and some ivory turtlenecks. Oh, and an eggshell silk short-sleeved blouse with the cutest tie at the neck. Dieter loves me in that," she confided. "He thinks it makes me look sexy."

A loud groan startled them. "*Dio mio,* Stefania, save the racy stories for your bachelorette party, will you?"

They both snickered at the typical brotherly response. But Renata returned to the dress subject quickly. "All of those whites you like to wear are actually not pure white. With your lovely coloring, you're attracted to ivories and off-whites. I think this pure white is washing you out."

"Oh. I thought it was the lighting."

"Nope, it's the fabric color." Renata had actually paid one of her lighting designer friends to install the most flattering light possible. "Wait here."

She ducked out of the cubicle. Giorgio looked up from his phone. Renata thought his interest would drop when he saw it was just her, but instead his gaze sharpened. "And which one of your dresses did you pick out for yourself?"

"For me?" She was flustered for a second. "I like all of them, but I've never needed one, I mean…"

"Your boyfriend hasn't, how do they say, popped the question?"

Exhilaration roared through her. "Boyfriend? What boyfriend?" She strutted into the stockroom, making sure her wiggle skirt lived up to its name.

3

GIORGIO FOUGHT TO KEEP the drool from shorting out his phone. Renata Pavoni was the sexiest woman he'd met in a long time, her dark blue eyes gleaming in a knowing manner. Even the tiny diamond decorating the side of her lovely straight nose turned him on. Like any real man, he loved curvy women instead of the unhealthy string-bean look. And the way she worked that round ass of hers under the tight skirt—*che bella ragazza*—what a beautiful girl. Like those old black-and-white movies his *nonna* liked, where the women's sultry eyes promised untold delights once their men removed their formfitting, low-cut dresses.

Removing Renata's clothing—opening her sheer black blouse, button by button. Peeling down—no, pushing up her tight red skirt to discover for himself if she was vintage down to the garter belt and hose.

The image of Renata's rich red hair spread out on his pillow as he kneeled over her was too much for his lonely, deprived cock, which immediately sprang to life.

Giorgio muttered a curse under his breath. Poor timing, to lose control in the middle of a wedding boutique with his sister only meters away. He peeled off his suit jacket and draped it over his lap, but then his phone buzzed—his assistant, Alessandro. *"Pronto,"* he answered.

"Signor, the investigator sent me a preliminary report on the person you requested."

"Ah, yes." Giorgio darted a guilty look at the dressing room, half expecting Stefania to come roaring out. *"Un momento,* Alessandro. I am going to step outside to talk." He leaped to his feet and headed for the front door, his jacket slung over his forearm. "Okay, give me the highlights and then send a copy to my phone."

"According to the report, the princess's fiancé, Dieter von Thalberg, was born to Graf Hans and Grafin Maria von Thalberg, Count and Countess of Thalberg, thirty years ago in Bavaria. He is heir to a large brewery on his mother's side as well as to the ancestral holdings on his father's."

"So he has money as long as the Germans drink beer—forever, I would think. Excellent." He'd heard enough horror stories from acquaintances about freeloaders marrying their sisters, breaking their hearts and then demanding large sums of money in exchange for not writing a sleazy tell-all book.

"Dieter von Thalberg is also the star forward for a big German football club." Alessandro's voice grew animated. "I didn't realize it was the same person—he uses a shortened version of his family name as a player. Three years ago he set the league record for goals scored. But since he turned thirty, he has not had as much playing time and was heavily recruited to come play for a team in New York, probably where he met the princess— *Signor,* why do the Americans call it soccer? I have always wondered. Anyway, the investigator will continue to look for any items in his past that would cause difficulties—previous marriages, illegitimate offspring, personal encounters with, um, professional ladies, videorecordings of a sexual nature, that sort of thing."

Giorgio winced. Stefania would kill him for sure if she found out he was investigating Dieter for prostitutes and sex tapes, but so be it. If the man had something to hide, better she knew sooner than later.

Renata opened the door and poked her head out. "Stefania wants you."

"Okay." He got off the phone and returned to the boutique.

"Sit." Renata pointed to the sofa and he complied. She could boss him around anytime. "Here comes the bride!" She swung the curtain aside and a glorious woman emerged. This couldn't be his baby sister. This young goddess glowed in a golden nimbus of light, her hair a dark cloud around her radiant face.

His jaw dropped. "Stefania?" he asked, as if Renata had exchanged her for another woman.

The vision giggled and broke the spell. "Of course, *stupido*—who elsc?"

"Wow, Stefania, you look—you look—" He was stammering now.

"Amazing," Renata supplied. "Pcrfect. Wonderful."

"Yes, yes, all of those." He rubbed a hand over his face. *Mamma mia,* when had she grown into such a beautiful woman? And he would be walking her down the Vinciguerra cathedral aisle to give her hand in holy matrimony to a thug footballer. He desperately wished his *nonna* were here, that his parents were still here on earth, but all he could do was muddle along on his own.

Renata seemed to sense his turmoil and glided toward his sister. "This is a tea-length satin dress with a portrait neckline and ruching down the front." He understood the satin dress part but that was about it.

"Look at all these cool petticoats, George." Stefania lifted her skirt and he winced, but all he saw was layers of fluffy fabric.

"Yes, um, very nice."

"Renata is going to edge a couple petticoats in gold satin ribbon so they catch the light when I turn. And she says her aunt is absolutely fabulous at embroidery and can decorate one with my and Dieter's initials. Don't you just love the color? Renata calls it *champagne*."

"But—it's not white." Giorgio was still thunderstruck by Stefania's womanly transformation and couldn't think of anything to say but the obvious.

His sister shrugged. "Princess Diana didn't wear a white dress, either—hers was ivory." Renata circled her, pulling at the fabric to check the fit.

"Yes, and *Nonna* always said look what happened to *that* marriage."

She stabbed a slender finger at him. "Stop it, Giorgio! The Princess was very kind to me at Mamma and Papa's funeral."

Renata dropped a handful of satin and stared at them. "Wait—Princess Diana came to your parents' funeral?"

Giorgio and Stefania exchanged glances and faced her. Giorgio spoke first. "Yes, she did, and you're right, Stefania. She was kind to both of us."

"I didn't tell Renata about our family, George." Stefania blinked rapidly. "I just wanted to be a regular bride looking at dresses without any fanfare or fuss."

"Tell me what?" Renata folded her arms across her magnificent chest.

"We should introduce ourselves again, Stefania, don't you think?" Giorgio bowed again, hoping that the truth wouldn't send the woman screaming out the door or straight to the tabloids. "May I present my sister Stefania Maria

Cristina Angela Martelli di Leone, *principessa di* Vinciguerra and I am Giorgio Alphonso Paolo Martelli di Leone, *il principe* di Vinciguerra."

"Come on, every bride is a princess on her wedding day, but you—you're a real princess?"

His sister nodded. "But it's a small country, really. Giorgio hardly needs to do anything to keep it running."

He glared at his sister—now Renata would think he was a brainless dilettante. She wore a peculiar expression as it was. "So you're a prince? Correct me if I'm wrong, but Italy is a republic now."

"Our grandmother, Giorgio and I make up the royal family of Vinciguerra, which is one of only two principalities on the Italian peninsula that wasn't taken over when Italy unified in the 1800s," Stefania explained glibly, having given the history lecture many times before. "The rest of the small duchies and kingdoms were absorbed into the greater Italian republic—but not ours. Our father was the Crown Prince, and now Giorgio's got the gig."

His slacker-prince/do-nothing gig. "Yes, I do my best. I do apologize, Signorina Renata, if we have not been up front with you from the beginning, but it is difficult to know if someone will call the infernal paparazzi. They can be very unpleasant."

"Like when Mamma and Papa died."

Giorgio's face hardened into grim lines, remembering the brokenhearted little girl who had sobbed into his chest for years after the awful loss. "So far those jackals do not know about Stefania's engagement, but they will find out eventually."

"Not from me, they won't!" Renata's eyes snapped, her New York accent thickening.

"Of course not," Stefania defended her. "But once they know that I am getting my wedding dress from you, they will not give you a moment's rest. It will be good for your business, though," she added quickly. "Lots of publicity."

"Oh." Renata obviously hadn't considered that aspect, and he appreciated it. "I never blab about our clients and I'll make sure my aunt doesn't, either."

"We appreciate it, Renata." Stefania hugged her, and Giorgio wished he could do the same.

"So this is the dress you want, Stefania?"

His sister turned to him, her eyes shining. "Oh, yes, George, I love it. I know it's shorter than what Vinciguerran brides usually wear, but won't it look lovely in the cathedral with its marble and gold decorations?"

"You will look lovely." He cupped her shoulders and kissed her on the forehead. His eyes watered a bit—had to be the Brooklyn air. He faced Renata, who wore a knowing smile on her red lips. "We'd like to get this dress—perfect for a princess."

"Absolutely." Renata hustled Stefania over to the trifold mirror and they baffled Giorgio with their discussion of fabric options, cuts and embellishments. His only contribution was his credit card once Stefania went to change into her regular clothing.

He blinked at the total on the slip—surely all that fine custom work had to cost more. He glanced up at Renata. "That's all?"

She put her hands on her hips. "Did you expect me to mark it up just because you're this, this royalty thing?"

"Yes," he answered truthfully.

"Then those other shop owners are scumbags. You should find someplace better."

He pushed the signed slip toward her. "I believe we have."

A faint flush crept up her neckline into her cheeks. She

busied herself by shutting down the computer and fussing with a stack of papers.

"You are finished for the day?"

She glanced over her shoulder at a black cat clock with a swinging tail. "I'm meeting my friend at the art school to see a new student exhibit."

Stefania burst out of the dressing room. "And I have class in an hour, George. Can you take me back to Manhattan?"

"Of course." Stefania inexplicably refused to use the car service most of the time in favor of the subway but she was in a hurry. "And, Signorina Renata, are you going to Manhattan, as well?"

"Well, yes, but I don't want to inconvenience you."

"No inconvenience." Stefania tugged on her short wool coat and belted it. "Come on, it'll be fun." Her merry gaze darted between her brother and her dress designer.

Giorgio gave her a neutral smile. So his little sister had picked up on his attraction to Renata and was playing matchmaker. She was in love, ergo, the whole world should be in love. He was a grown man—he knew better. Love was for fresh young girls and foolish young men.

"If you're sure." Renata wrapped herself in a black trench coat, her red lips and hair heating him up. She looked like a sensual spy from a war movie—the brave secret agent who arrives at her contact's apartment one foggy night, wearing her trench coat and nothing else. Or maybe in a corset and that black garter belt he'd imagined earlier...

"George? George!" Stefania was already at the door. "Renata's waiting for you so she can set the alarm."

Grateful he still carried his suit coat in front of him, Giorgio hurried to the door. Paolo must have been watching because he pulled the black limo up to the curb within seconds, coming around to open the doors for them.

"Renata, you sit in back with George. I want to visit with

Paolo since I haven't seen him in months." Stefania again, with part two of her plot. Visit with Paolo? The man put lie to the stereotype that all Italians were chatty. Giorgio would be surprised if Paolo spoke a dozen words a day.

Renata of course didn't know this and slid into the leather backseat and the big car fought its way through traffic to the Brooklyn Bridge, one of his favorite New York landmarks.

Renata tucked her shapely legs to the side as she stared up at the stone towers and steel cables. "It's amazing how well built the bridge is for being so old."

Giorgio smiled. His country still had remnants of ancient Roman bridges, but the Brooklyn Bridge was old by American standards.

Renata's phone buzzed and she reached into her handbag to check the text display. "Oh, darn. My friend Flick had some bad Thai food last night and can't make it to the gallery." She replied to the text and put away the phone.

"Flick?"

Renata grinned. "Her real name is Felicity, but it wasn't edgy enough for her as an up-and-coming artist with turquoise streaks in her hair. She told me to go ahead and she'd catch the exhibit some other time."

Giorgio mentally consigned all the business activities he had planned to the trash heap. "I would be happy to take you to the exhibit. I have no plans for the afternoon."

"Are you sure?" Her lips pursed thoughtfully.

He sneaked a look at Stefania, who was chattering away in Italian to Paolo, who nodded occasionally. He didn't want to let her know that he was going along with her scheming. "I would enjoy doing so."

"In that case, Giorgio, I'd be happy to show you around."

"My pleasure." It was the pleasure of spending time

with her, but he didn't want to come on too strong. "I am Vinciguerran—we love beautiful works of art. All kinds." Especially the one sitting next to him.

4

GIORGIO HATED THE ART—if he even thought of it as art. Renata wasn't convinced from the sideways glance out of the corner of her eye. Scary how well she could read him after only meeting him this morning. He had sent his beefy driver back to their hotel.

"And this signifies…" He gestured elegantly at the smelly mess of vegetation on the floor.

She peered at the information tag. "The broken cornstalks and soybean plants tell the plight of the family farmer in the ever-growing domination of industrial agriculture."

He blinked. "Ah." Giorgio was a good sport, though, examining what looked like his *nonna's* compost heap.

"Let's see the next." She slipped her hand into the crook of his elbow to tug him to another dubious installation. Lovely. A tangle of rusty barbed wire. Her heel caught on the rough concrete floor and he steadied her.

"Careful, Renata. I do not want to take you for a tetanus shot." He smiled down at her and she forgot for a second that he was an honest-to-God prince of someplace in Italy and his suit cost more than she made in a year. No, when he smiled at her, he was just Mr. Hot Guy who made her want to shred that expensive suit off him with her teeth.

Her breathing sped up, pressing her breasts into the nice bodice of her black blouse.

He noticed, his fingers tightening on hers. Not so cool on the inside, then. "And this represents the tangle of modern life?"

"No, the plight of refugees."

Giorgio nodded. "Stefania is patroness of a charity for women and children that often works with refugee and displaced families."

"At her age?" Stefania wasn't much younger than Renata.

"Since she was thirteen." His tone was full of love and admiration. "She testified in front of the United Nations High Commissioner for Refugees when she was nineteen. Stefania has become a better strategist since then. Perhaps I should have discouraged her from studying political science, but when a twelve-year-old reads Machiavelli's *The Prince* so she can pass political tips on to her older brother, what else would I expect?"

Renata let him guide her along to the next exhibit. It was a video installation with a variety of blurry faces grimacing in turn as loud static played in the background. Giorgio regarded it with the same pleasant expression he'd pasted on his face as soon as they'd walked in. He really was a polished man.

Renata went up on tiptoe to whisper in his ear. "This is just awful. Do you mind if we leave now?"

"Aren't you enjoying yourself." His eyes twinkled.

"You'll know when I'm enjoying myself," she assured him.

"Indeed?" He turned his head slowly so their faces were almost touching. Renata swallowed hard. She thought he was going to kiss her but he clenched his jaw instead. Perhaps public displays of affection were against the Vinciguerran Royal Book of Etiquette. "I will call Paolo to pick us up."

"No, don't." She didn't want anyone intruding in what was turning out to be a very intriguing afternoon. "It's a nice day—let's walk."

"Where?"

"A surprise." She tugged him out of the gallery and onto the sidewalk, tipping her face up. "Ah, sun. Makes up for a long and gloomy winter."

"An Italian girl like you should always get plenty of sun."

She patted her jaw. "Bad for the complexion. The rest of my family has the typical dark hair and olive skin like you, but I only burn."

"No wonder you have such lovely skin. You must be careful when you travel to Italy the next time. You know our sun can be very strong."

"The next time? I've never been to Italy before."

He stopped and stared down at her. "Your name is Renata Pavoni and you've never visited Italy? How can that be?"

She laughed and led him along the busy street. "My parents have five of us. You've never priced out airfare to Europe for seven, but my mother did once. We heard her scream of shock down the street."

Giorgio looked momentarily startled—budget concerns didn't cross his radar. He nodded thoughtfully. "What part of Italy did your family come from?"

"After the war, my grandparents on my mom's side came from a little village on the Italian Riviera called Corniglia. My *nonna* says the town is perched on a huge rock surrounded by grapevines. They make this special kind of wine found nowhere else in the world."

"Scciachetrà."

"Yeah, that's right. We crack open a bottle every New Year's Eve to toast the old country." Renata shivered in remembrance. "Boy, is that stuff strong. Made of raisins, so the sugar is very concentrated."

"I've never tried it, although we have something similar in Vinciguerra, called Bocca di Leone—The Lion's Mouth. We serve it in thimble-size glasses and no one can drink more than a few without falling over." He sighed. "I'll have to make sure we have enough for Stefania's wedding. It's the traditional toast for weddings, especially royal weddings."

"And you are the di Leone family, after all."

"Our ancestors invented it." He grinned down at her. "I may need a couple stiff drinks before I walk Stefania down the aisle."

"Buck up, Giorgio." She patted his arm. "Everyone gets a bit misty-eyed when they give the bride away. Which sword and medals will you be wearing?"

Giorgio gave her a sidelong look. "Sometimes I cannot tell if you are joking with me or not."

"That's because you are much too serious." She gestured. "Look at the beautiful day! Here we are in the most fabulous city in the world, we have lovely Central Park over there, the sun is shining, your sister has her wedding dress and you didn't have a nervous breakdown trying to shop for one. Do you know how rare it is to keep good mental health shopping for a bridal gown?"

"Um, no."

"When I worked at a regular bridal salon, fits of hysteria, therapeutic slapping and tranquilizers of dubious legality were an everyday occurrence."

"It seems I've dodged the bullet."

"You sure have. Hey, let's cut through the park."

HE TOOK A DEEP BREATH of the spring-scented air, the pale green leaves on the trees unfolding from their winter's rest.

The tension started to leave his muscles, although they were still mighty buff.

"See? All you needed was a nice little nature walk. I bet it's been a long time since you got outdoors for some fresh air. A guy like you isn't meant to be cooped up indoors pushing paperwork all day. Maybe you should get yourself a yacht—I mean if you don't already have one—"

"We have my father's yacht. We loan it out to people for field trips and marine science expeditions."

"Weddings, proms and bar mitzvahs."

He grinned. "Probably, if anybody requested it."

"Don't you or your sister ever use it?"

"Stefania does for her charity fundraisers." They passed near a tree and he held a branch back that might have scratched her face.

"Not for that, but for your personal use."

He shook his head. "Not since she started at the university and I took over more duties from my grandmother."

"All work and no play makes Giorgio a dull boy," she quoted the old saying. Imagine owning a yacht and being too busy to use it. Running even a small country must take an enormous amount of time.

"Then I should stop being so dull."

He pulled her to the side of the path underneath a big oak tree. "Is that red lipstick smudge-proof?"

"Yeah, pretty much. It actually has a sealant clear gloss that—"

"Good," he cut her off. Wow, for a prince he needed some work on conversational manners.

He kissed her.

And he did *not* need some work on his kissing. Renata's mouth fell open in shock and he took advantage, slipping his tongue between her hopefully smudge-proof lips. She clutched his broad shoulders as he caressed her mouth with his, gently nibbling and sucking at her lips.

Renata had never been kissed like this, with passion and lust but tenderness, too. Her previous boyfriends had been younger than Giorgio, in their early or mid-twenties, and had either been tentative in their kisses or overly aggressive, mashing her lips as if to prove their desire. Now Giorgio was planting kisses across her jaw and holy crap— he licked her neck's equivalent of a G-spot and she nearly screamed with pleasure.

His hot breath quickened against her skin and she knew he was as on fire as she was. "Mmm, Renata." He lifted his head.

Renata's eyes fluttered open when she realized he wasn't kissing her anymore. "Wow."

He wore a dazed look on his face, as well. At least she wasn't the only one. She probably would have socked him if he'd been gloating. "I am sorry, Renata."

"Sorry for kissing me?" She shoved him away and plopped her hands on her hips.

"Never. Sorry for pushing you against a tree and kissing you in public." His lips were plump from kisses but her lipstick had lived up to its promise.

She wanted to taste his mouth again—hell, taste him all over. "You'd rather kiss me in private?" She traced her finger up his golden silk tie.

Giorgio caught her hand in his and pressed a kiss to the palm. "I would like nothing more."

A handful of female runners clattered along the path next to them, all of them ogling Giorgio. He turned away, not wanting to be recognized.

He rubbed his face. "Much as I'd like to invite you to my suite at the Plaza—"

"You have a suite at the Plaza?" she interrupted. "Is it as fancy as in the movies? I've only been in the lobby once."

"I don't know about the movies, my rooms are very nice. But…"

"Too fast, isn't it?" she asked ruefully. Despite her brassy attitude, Renata didn't want to hop into bed with a guy an hour after she met him. Well, she did, but she wouldn't.

He nodded solemnly. "Paolo hasn't had time to do a background check on you."

She squawked in indignation and socked him in the arm.

"Ow!" He clutched his arm and laughed. "Renata, I'm just kidding. It's too fast because I want to get to know you better."

"Good answer." She stood on her tiptoes and kissed his cheek. And although she wanted Giorgio pretty badly, he came with miles and miles of strings attached—business, money and the fact that he had his own country. Maybe it would be best to leave it at a quick kiss. A hot, wet, tongue-tangling kiss on a romantic spring afternoon in the most romantic park in New York City.

Renata mentally slapped herself before she dragged Giorgio back behind that tree and did something to the man that started with *public* and ended with *indecency*. "What's next?" It was a bigger question than it seemed.

He took her hand again. "What would a beautiful New Yorker like to do on an unexpected afternoon away from work?"

Renata spotted a white gleam from beyond the leafy green trees. "How about the real art museum?"

"Whatever you'd like."

That wasn't an option. She dabbed at her mouth with a handkerchief. "How's my lipstick?"

"Lovely." He smiled down at her. "But I could make it smudge if I had enough time."

"I bet you could," she breathed. Darn it, he wasn't making this easy for her. "Come on, let's go."

RENATA LED GIORGIO UP the marble steps to the main entrance of the Metropolitan Museum of Art. He gazed up at the impressive multi-story facade along Fifth Avenue. "Stefania and I came here at least once a month while she was growing up. I haven't been since the cleaning and restoration several years ago. It's quite a dramatic change."

"The gray stone actually turned out to be white after all." The tall marble columns with elaborately carved tops and arched high windows looked like a Greek temple—a temple of art. "Are you sure you don't mind coming along for the historical costume exhibit? Most men aren't terribly interested in women's clothing—just how to undo them." She felt a flush rise in her cheeks.

He laughed at her bluntness and held out his elbow for her to take. She accepted and they started to climb the steep stairs. "But I am terribly interested in women's clothing. Didn't I prove that by flying all the way to New York to look at wedding dresses?"

"It was very sweet of you to come." She impulsively squeezed his upper arm. No give at all. His expensive Italian suit was covering an equally nice body.

"I try to do what Stefania tells me." Giorgio smiled at her. "The children's book where the brother and sister run away to live in this museum was her favorite as a girl. I was quite terrified she might try the same thing, so I brought her here whenever she asked me. If I couldn't, then my friends Jack and Frank did."

He held the door for Renata and they went to the ticket counter. "Two tickets for the museum and the costume exhibit," she told the museum employee, reaching into her purse for the money.

Giorgio put his hand over hers. "My treat, I insist." He reached for his slim wallet tucked into his jacket pocket.

"No, no, you're my guest." She went for her purse again.

"No." He gave a credit card to the employee who hastily swiped it through the reader before they could cause any more delay in her line.

Renata clamped her lips together and accepted her ticket. They went into the museum foyer and she pulled him aside. "Look, just because you are a prince and all doesn't mean I can't afford to pay for museum tickets."

He gave her a considering look. "You think I paid because I have much more money than you?"

"Yes."

"No." He took her hand. "I would pay for your ticket with the last money I owned because I'm a man and you're a beautiful woman who makes me laugh and enjoy myself. Unfortunately, that is a rare occurence for me."

"Oh, please." She made a dismissive gesture with her free hand.

"No, thank you." He caught her other hand. "I know I've had many advantages in my life, but free time isn't one of them."

"Same here." She squeezed his hands. He had said she was beautiful, so she'd cut him some slack. Well, a lot of slack.

"Let's not waste any of our precious time. Shall we go to the costume exhibit?"

"Absolutely. Then we can see whatever you'd like," she offered.

He offered her his arm again, and they followed the signs to the gallery. "I've already seen most of the regular collection, so your special exhibit sounds just fine."

"How about the arms and armor collection? Men always like that."

He sniffed disdainfully. "We have a much better collection at home."

"What? Better than the museum?"

"I'm just kidding." He nudged her playfully and she snorted.

"But you do have some arms and armor at your house."

"At the local museum," he clarified. "But the armor used to be at my house."

"You got tired of peasants wandering through looking at it?"

"If all peasants were as lovely as you, I would have no problem with that." She raised her eyebrows. "I'm only joking, Renata. I'm priviledged to serve my people, not the other way around."

"All right, then." She let him off the hook. For a prince, he wasn't very arrogant. Not that she knew very many. Or any.

He wrapped his arm around her shoulder and pointed to the gallery entrance. "Here we are."

Renata gave a gasp as she and Giorgio entered the darkened, dramatically lit hall. "Now this is what I call a real art exhibit." Strategically placed spotlights illuminated mannequins in elegant 1890's ballgowns.

"Very elegant," Giorgio agreed. "And little danger of tetanus."

Renata went as close to the mannequins as she could without getting tossed out of the museum and peered at the fine details of the gowns. They were satin, velvet and silk. The silhouette was a tight bodice flowing out to a small bustle and then fabric draping down to the floor in a small train. The embroidery was elaborately done with crystals, pearls and jet accents. Butterflies and flowers, swirls and loops. "Maybe I haven't been taking enough advantage of Aunt Barbara's skills. She could do this in her sleep."

"The lady who is going to embroider Stefania and Dieter's initials on her, um, underskirt?"

Renata laughed. Typical brother. "That's her. She'll be disappointed she missed you." The overwhelming understatement of the century. A real live prince and princess came to out-of-the-way Peacock Designs and Aunt Barbara was sitting in the gastroenterologist's waiting room. She'd at least get to meet Stefania when she came for her fittings.

The next rooms had sports clothing, a revolutionary idea in the late nineteenth century. Although playing tennis in a floor-length dress or riding a bicycle in a wool skirt and suitjacket didn't appeal to Renata, she saw the historical importance of the broadening of women's activities.

Ah, more ball gowns, but this time they were a flowing, turn-of-the-century style with Asian-influenced fasteners and draping tunic silhouettes. Another set of new ideas for her.

"Art Nouveau, one of my favourite eras." Giorgio gazed at the Tiffany stained-glass windows and classic Italian opera posters.

"Oh, my God, me, too! I just love Gustav Klimt's painting with the man and woman embracing surrounded by all that gold and jewel tones."

"The Kiss." His gaze dropped to her lips.

She licked her mouth, suddenly dry. "Yes, it's called *The Kiss.*"

"Have you been to Vienna to see it?" he asked.

She laughed and the spell was broken—at least temporarily. "No, I haven't made it to Vienna yet." Or anywhere east of the Atlantic Ocean.

"You should go."

With what money? She caught his hand and pulled him along. He was a sweet guy, but there was a world of difference—and money—between them. "Maybe someday. Oh, look at the suffragettes' uniforms. Very masculine."

Giorgio stood patiently next to her, not fidgeting a bit or checking his phone as she examined the clothing in the remaining rooms. She wished she could take photos, but the light was too low to get any of the details. They exited into a gift shop with several reproduction jewelry items and books on art and fashion of the time period covered.

Giorgio picked up the hardcover, full-color photo book that accompanied the exhibit. "Would you allow me to buy you a small gift, a souvenir of our afternoon together?"

"That book's not exactly small." But she was dying to get her hands on it, especially to look at the beading and embroidery in close detail.

"I'll carry it for you if it's too heavy." His green eyes twinkled.

She paused for a second and then decided her self-reliance could take a backseat to graciousness for once. "That would be lovely. Thank you."

Giorgio seemed surprised, as if he'd expected her to tussle with him over it. "You're welcome." He hastened to the cash register to pay for it before she changed her mind, probably.

Renata busied herself by examining the jewelry. It was a bit elaborate for her tastes, with filigree and crystals and jet beads galore. Aunt Barbara would love it.

"Do you see anything you like here?" he asked.

She shook her head. "I was just thinking my aunt would like some of this. She likes more...elaborate things than I do."

He eyed her up and down. "A woman who looks like a forties' movie star doesn't think that counts as elaborate?"

"I suppose silk stockings with seams up the back can't be considered plain."

"Not at all." His voice sounded husky for a second. "But authentic, right?"

"Absolutely." Renata had to clear her own throat. "Maybe I'll bring Aunt Barbara to see the exhibit. I've encouraged her to branch out a bit with some designs of her own."

"With you as her mentor, I'm sure it would be a success."

"That's kind of you."

Giorgio shrugged. "Only the truth. You're a self-made woman, whereas I'm the royal caretaker, making sure everything stays intact for the next generation." He sounded a bit dejected.

"But that's important, too. You have thousands of families depending on you to make sure everything runs smoothly, that parents can give their children the opportunities to succeed that they might not have had themselves."

He grinned. "You've very smart, you know that?"

"Of course. And now, if you'll call for that slick car of yours we can tour around for a bit before you meet your sister for dinner."

He immediately texted his driver who showed up in an impossibly short period of time. Giorgio helped her into the limo. "Drive downtown, Paolo."

Paolo nodded and they slid away from the curb. Renata settled back into the luxurious seats. She didn't know where the royal ride was going, but she was sure it would be memorable.

"THANK YOU FOR DINNER, Renata." Giorgio relaxed back into the limo seat. "I have to admit I am not used to ladies paying for me."

"Don't be silly, it was just a chili dog," she chided him. She hadn't been in a limo since one of her brothers' weddings, and this was much nicer than being stuffed into the back with several giddy bridesmaids in poufy dresses. "I'll add it onto the alterations bill for your sister's dress if you insist."

He leaned toward her. "I do."

Stefania had called to cancel dinner since she had a term paper due soon and her fiancé was fogged in at Heathrow airport anyway.

Giorgio had called his driver to come get them and they had cruised the city as best as they could with a giant limo. But it was getting late, and Renata had reluctantly told Giorgio to head for Brooklyn.

"Tell me when you are free again." Giorgio twined his fingers between hers.

"Free for what?"

"Free to see me again. I'll take you to the Plaza for dinner."

She rested her head on his shoulder. "Only if they serve chili dogs."

"I'll make sure they do." He ran the back of his hand along her cheek. "I want to see you again."

Oh, so did she. "Would you like to see my neighborhood?"

"What?" He looked out the window at the identical row houses stretching as far as they could see.

"Tell your driver to cruise around in this area for a little while. I'll give you a private tour." She was practically crawling out of her skin with lust and finally gave in.

He pressed an intercom button and gave instructions in Italian. "There. He will drive around until I tell him to stop. He cannot see or hear anything in the back so you can feel free to say whatever you want." He pressed a button that turned on hidden dim lighting. "I want to see you while we talk. You are the sexiest woman I have ever met."

She snorted.

"What?" He furrowed his black brows. "You do not think you are sexy?"

"Oh, I know I am." And that had been hard-won self-knowledge. "But I'm no six-foot, one-hundred-pound supermodel."

"Thank God," he said fervently. "I'm not a man who likes women with more muscle than me." He caressed her cheek. "A real man wants a real woman, soft and smooth." He trailed his hand down her neck to her shoulder. "Round and ripe, like a juicy peach plucked from the tree."

Renata was ready to be plucked, backseat of the car or not. Her nipples were as hard as peach pits inches from where his fingers stroked the base of her neck and her "fruit juices" were definitely ready for sampling. "And you are a real man, Giorgio," she purred.

"You know I am, Renata."

"Tell me what you think of me—all real, by the way." She sat back and slowly unbuttoned her blouse, her eyes never leaving his. He swallowed hard as her black lace bra appeared.

"Bella, che bella." Still he hesitated, so she shrugged the blouse off her shoulders.

"All for you, Giorgio." She unfastened her French twist and shook her red hair loose like a pinup girl. "I've been waiting all day for your touch. Don't make me wait anymore. You don't want to get a reputation for a tease, do you?"

He groaned, his cock stretching his Italian wool pants in a way the designers never intended. She crawled over to him and cupped his erection. His green eyes practically rolled back into his head. He was huge even through the cloth, his plump head firm and round under her fingers. The thought of all that Italian goodness inside her made her shiver. She started to unzip him.

The next second she was flat on her back on the seat, her bra gone and her breasts bare. His mouth was firmly fastened to one nipple, his fingers playing with the other. He sucked on her as if he were starving for her, and she was starving for him. She arched her back, pushing her breast up for his easier access.

He switched to the other breast, leaving her nipple moist and swollen in the cool air. She shivered and hardened even further.

So did he, his cock pressing against her inner thigh. She wiggled under him and he lifted his glossy black head. "You make me crazy."

"Then go crazy with me."

"Not yet." He slid his hand up her thigh and stopped. "Ah, *Dio mio,* you are wearing *giarretterre*—I do not know the word in English."

"Garters," she supplied. "I'm glad you like them."

"I love them," he said hoarsely. He caressed the slice of thigh between her panties and stockings and cupped her bare ass. "A thong? You are going to set me off like a rocket and I have not even seen you yet."

He shimmied her skirt up around her waist and stared down at her in rapture. "Look at you. So beautiful."

Renata looked down at herself. Her lower half could be described charitably as curvy and fat by several skinny bitches she'd run into over the years.

He kissed her soft belly and she jumped at the ticklish sensation. He grinned up at her. "You give up another secret to me, Renata. You are ticklish."

"You just startled me," she informed him loftily and jumped a second time when he darted his tongue into her navel.

"And again?" He made circular tracks with his tongue,

widening out from her belly button and down to the tiny black ribbon at the top of her thong.

"Well, yes."

As he nuzzled the ribbon, his breath was hot on her belly. He hooked the front panel of her thong and pulled it free. "Are you ticklish here?" He slid his finger between her folds and zoomed in on her clit.

Her back bowed as he lazily circled that greedy bit of flesh and all she could do was groan.

"If you don't like it, I can stop."

Renata smiled at his blather and her eyes rolled back in her head as he lowered his mouth to her thong. With his tongue he caressed her clit, soft and wet at first and then harder as he pressed her with its tip. Her legs fell apart and she gave herself up to his tongue. His big hands had gone right where he wanted, cupping and molding her ass with fervor and appreciation.

Then her mind shut off and her body took over. Or Giorgio took over her body. His five o'clock shadow rasped her inner thighs but his lips were gentle as he drew her clit into his mouth and sucked.

Her fingernails left marks in the soft leather upholstery. Anticipation raced up her belly into her breasts, tightening her nipples even further. She rolled them between her fingers, earning a groan of approval from Giorgio as he raised his head to watch her.

Her brazenness inspired him and he dived back down—this time slipping a finger inside her as he licked her. She immediately clamped down around him. He slid in and out, adding a second finger and flicking her clit hard with his tongue.

Renata propped herself up on her elbows to get a better look at Giorgio. Seeing him even added to her arousal. She was dying, panting, sweating—and loved it. Spread open wide in the backseat of a limo with a man she'd met less than twelve hours earlier going to town on her, his face slick with her juices and his Egyptian cotton shirt damp with sweat.

He pulled his fingers out and stuck his tongue inside her. She collapsed back on the seat, her insides pulsing around his tongue in some dimly remembered but familiar feeling. "Oh, yes, Giorgio. Oh, just like that…" She slapped her hand over her mouth as her moans increased in volume.

He held her tight despite her body's frantic movements, knowing she was very close. He moved his mouth back to her clit and that was enough for her. Pleasure from his mouth shot all through her body, her head whipping back and forth as she fought back a scream of pure delight.

On and on the sweet torture went until she was too limp to do anything but finally put a hand on his head. He lifted his face and gave a satisfied smirk. "What, no more?"

"I am all done, and you know it." Renata was glad the limo driver didn't hit any potholes because she would have slid bonelessly off the seat. On the other hand, she was so floppy she wouldn't be injured. She struggled to her elbows. "My God, Giorgio, where did you learn to do that?"

He moved to sit back on the seat, sighing in relief as he stretched out his back and shoulders. He pulled her to his lap and she noticed he was just as aroused as before. "A trip through the fleshpots of Europe, of course," he enunciated with a perfect upper-crust British accent.

She cracked up. He sounded like the leading man of a Masterpiece Theatre miniseries but was probably telling her the truth. "Sounds like a fun trip to me."

"This trip is much better," he assured her, caressing her bare breasts. They both sighed in pleasure as he cupped the heavy weight, lazily brushing her nipple with his thumb. "Renata, you have the most perfect body. *Le tette bellissimas.*"

She gasped in mock horror. "Why, Prince Giorgio! Such slang from your royal lips." He had told her she had beautiful tits.

"You understand that slang? Then how about this? *Ti voglio fare l'amore questa notte.*"

"You want to make love to me tonight."

"There is always the Plaza," he offered.

Renata glanced at the small digital clock in the back of the partition and almost cried with disappointment. "Is it so late already?"

Giorgio stroked her knee. "Is that a problem?"

She nodded. "I have an appointment at seven tomorrow morning."

He groaned. "Why so early?"

"The bride has a last-minute business trip and it's the week before her wedding. These high-powered brides can be a lot of work."

"Lucky for Stefania that you are so conscientious." He raised her hand to his lips and kissed her knuckles. "Tell me when you are free and I will be waiting on your doorstep."

"How about now?" She certainly hadn't minded the backseat atmosphere.

He looked tempted for a second but shook his head. "I am selfish. What I have in mind will take more time than Paolo has gas in the tank. And if I let you touch me, we will be parked at the side of the road making the limo rock while Paolo walks to a gas station."

She didn't doubt for one second that Giorgio could go for hours, judging from what was poking her through his pants. But, oh, what was she missing tonight? Stupid high-powered bride.

It took all of her willpower to decline his offer but she needed to be alert for her appointment since that bride was a live wire at best and out-of-control crazy at worst. "I'm sorry I can't go to the hotel with you, but I have to get at least a few hours' sleep. My client is difficult and I need my wits about me."

He flopped back onto the car seat. "Duty first. Unfortunately I understand."

"Thank you." She cupped his jaw and kissed him slowly and passionately until they were both breathing hard again.

He suddenly jerked away from her. "Stop that. Or else I will not wait until tomorrow."

Renata grinned. "It is tomorrow. Almost one-thirty."

"Ah, better. Then I will see you later today. That sounds much better." He programmed his number into her phone and took her number. "That is my private line. Only my family and my personal assistant have that number."

"Wow." She checked her phone's display and he had programmed his name in as *G.*

He smiled at her. "We try to guard our privacy but it doesn't always work out."

"I won't let this fall into the wrong hands," she promised.

"I know you won't." He kissed the tip of her nose, surprising Renata with the pure affection behind the gesture.

Her surroundings finally caught her eye. "Oh, we're a block from my place. Turn left at the next light." She directed Giorgio and he relayed the directions to his driver.

"I'm going to ask you to park here around the corner. Many of my neighbors are elderly insomniacs and me pulling up in a limo this time of night will only further convince them I'm a woman of dubious morals."

"I will testify on your behalf that your morals are not nearly as dubious as I would prefer."

She choked with laughter and slapped him in the chest. "Somehow I don't think they would believe you." He looked dangerously sexy with his shirt yanked out of his waistband, his hair mussed and a glittering look of barely suppressed lust in his green eyes.

"Pity." The limo stopped and he handed her out of the door. "I will walk you to your door."

Her neighborhood was fairly safe but she wanted to drag out every moment with him that she could. He constantly glanced around them and inspected her dark exterior basement entrance for any stray wino or mugger. The only man she wanted to take advantage of her was standing beside her. "All clear."

She unlocked her door and was struck by a weird wave of awkwardness. "Well…thank you for everything." That should cover it. Wedding dresses, art museums, chili dogs, heavy petting in the limo backseat—what a wild day.

He drew her into his arms. "Don't thank me, Renata. I owe you much more than a dinner. Your dress has made Stefania extremely happy and meeting you has made me extremely happy, as well." He lowered his head and kissed her lips softly. "Until later, Renata. I'll call you later in the morning after your appointment."

She hated to leave him but a big yawn escaped her mouth.

Giorgio smiled and shooed her into her place. "Go, get some sleep. I can take a hint."

"Fine." She floated into the tiny entryway and locked the door behind her. Once he was sure she was tucked away, he gave a wave and took the steps two at a time up to street level.

Renata glided to her bathroom and gazed at her reflection. Her hair was tousled, her blouse was buttoned crook-

edly and her face was flushed. So was her mouth, her lipstick smeared.

She grinned. Giorgio was a man who kept his promises.
Given enough time and effort, he had smeared her smear-
proof lipstick.

5

GIORGIO WET HIS HANDKERCHIEF and cleaned his mouth of traces of Renata's lipstick, a wide smile reflected in the small mirror in the backseat. The day certainly hadn't turned out the way he'd expected, but he took pride in the fact that he had been smart enough to take the opportunity of getting to know Renata.

Especially since Stefania had accused him of being a, what was the American expression? Ah, yes, a stuffed shirt. The girl certainly had a way with words, much to his chagrin. Perhaps his day-to-day duties had encouraged a certain amount of rigidity—and not the good kind.

He laughed out loud. Oh, the tabloids would laugh if they saw what his true life was like. The Crown Prince sneaking around and making out in the backseat of a car like some teenager, stopping his pursuit of passion because of his archaic ideas of proper behavior. He already went further than he intended with the lovely Renata, but her words and body had urged him on past his good sense.

Stuffed shirt, hah! He rubbed his chest—no stuffing needed thanks to dutiful workouts, but maybe a bit sore. He took a deep breath and his muscles loosened a bit.

The Brooklyn Bridge loomed overhead and they sped

over it for the second time in a day. It was impressive, young or not. These Americans had an eye for design, he admitted to himself. Whether it was the bridge or Stefania's dress, New Yorkers knew how to make things work.

He patted his chest again—heartburn from that damned chili dog? He pressed a button to roll down the partition. "Have any antacids, Paolo?"

"You are ill, *signore?*"

"No, I don't think so." He chewed the chalky discs Paolo found for him and chased it down with a bottle of water. He closed his eyes, feeling Paolo's worried gaze on him. Not to worry, the worst thing he had going was a bit of indigestion and a massive case of blue balls. And yes, he'd known that American phrase all on his own.

They weaved through Manhattan traffic toward the hotel and Giorgio felt every bump. This was not good. The antacids hadn't helped a bit and he was starting to sweat.

Agonizing pain ripped through his chest up into his shoulder and down his arm. Dear God, was he having a heart attack? His sister's face flashed to mind, strangely followed by Renata's. Stevie he understood, but Renata? Stevie needed him—her only brother. And Renata—he needed her and he'd only met her.

It felt like a fist was squeezing his heart. He couldn't help groaning.

"Signor! Signor! Are you all right?"

Giorgio looked up at Paolo's panicked face and spoke with a calmness he didn't feel. "I don't think so, Paolo. Get me to the hospital."

"MR. MARTELLI? I'M DR. WEISS." Young and skinny with glasses, the E.R. physician was in need of a shave but looked awake enough.

Giorgio extended his hand, IV tubing dangling from his arm. "I am George and this is my friend Paul."

Dr. Weiss laughed. "And where are John and Ringo?"

Ah, a jokester. Giorgio suppressed a sigh. He guessed working in a New York City emergency department was grim enough that even the doctors tried to lighten things up.

"*Chè dice?* What is he saying?" Paolo asked in Italian.

"*Niente*—nothing. A Beatles joke," Giorgio replied in the same language.

"A joke? He dares joke with the Crown Prince of Vinciguerra when he is ill?" Paolo had no sense of humor under normal circumstances, and a doctor who thought he was a comedian was not helping.

Giorgio gestured for him to calm down. "This place is sad enough, Paolo. It is harmless."

Paolo subsided, but stared hard at the doc, who cleared his throat and got down to business.

"Okay, Mr. Martelli, I got your lab and EKG results back. The good news is, you're not having a heart attack. We think you had a major attack of indigestion, probably from those chili dogs you mentioned."

Giorgio blew out a sigh of relief. He had avoided the one thing he feared for himself. He quickly translated for Paolo, who crossed himself in thanks.

Dr. Weiss continued, "But the bad news is, I don't know why you haven't had one already. You look like a sixty-year-old man on paper. A sick sixty-year-old man."

His stomach churned. He was only thirty years old—what the hell was going on?

"You have a family history of heart disease?"

Oh, no, not that. He blinked rapidly. "Yes, my father."

"Okay." The doctor nodded. "It can run in the family. Your good cholesterol is down, your bad cholesterol is sky-high, your entire body is in a state of silent inflammation and your blood pressure when you got here about blew the top of your head off. It's minimally improved since we got your pain under control."

He muttered to Paolo what the doctor said. Paolo drew in a shocked breath. "So what do you recommend?"

"I don't know what you do for a living but you need to take some time off to get your health under control. Get to your primary care doctor and get a note if your boss gives you any grief. You have a primary care doctor?"

Giorgio nodded. "Yes, yes, I will see him as soon as I get home." He had been neglectful—it had been over three years since his last checkup.

"I mean it. I see young, strong guys like you all the time roll in here grabbing their chests. Sometimes they only roll out in a box, *capeesh?*" His Italian accent was straight out of *The Godfather,* but Giorgio understood all too well.

"I understand."

"Good." Dr. Weiss extended a hand and Giorgio shook it. "Watch your diet—more fruits, vegetables, lean meats and a splash of olive oil. Cut back on the pasta, bread and sweets. A glass or two a day of red wine is actually good for you, but no more than that. You don't want to rev up your liver on top of everything. Any questions?"

He had a million questions—like how fate could be so cruel as to start him along the same path as his father, but Dr. Weiss had no answer for that—no one did. "No, and thank you."

The doc left and Giorgio dropped his head back onto the hard gurney, covering his eyes with his forearm. He didn't want to be in the hospital, didn't want to have this sword hanging over his head. What if he hadn't eaten those damned chili dogs with Renata and instead had gone along his blissfully ignorant way until he dropped dead on the street, his office or God forbid, driving along the mountainous roads of Vinciguerra?

What would happen to Stefania if he died? She would have to run Vinciguerra alone once their grandmother passed away.

He swallowed hard and felt a beefy hand on his shoulder. "*Signore.* You will be all right—I promise."

"*Grazie,* Paolo." He removed his hand and sat up. A prince of Vinciguerra did not swoon and cry like a Victorian maiden. "We leave out the back door. I don't want anyone to know about this, especially the princess."

Paolo nodded. "I will bring the car to a side door."

Giorgio changed into his own clothing and met Paolo at the agreed-upon door. He slid into the backseat of the limo and closed his eyes. "Back to the hotel, Paolo."

He would make himself healthy again so that he could walk Stevie down the aisle, hand her off to that German footballer and watch his nieces and nephews come along. She had always wanted a large family after being so lonely as a child.

He had been lonely, too—a nineteen-year-old university student in New York raising an eleven-year-old girl. He had wanted to set a good example for her and spent much of his time with her instead of freely dating like other men his age. And despite what his sister had told Renata, running Vinciguerra did take a good deal of time. Was he still lonely?

Yes, but not when he was with Renata. He'd met her less than twelve hours ago and aside from his terror-filled medical emergency, she had occupied his thoughts ever since. Her sarcastic New York wit, her talent for handling his sister. And more personal memories, like how her mouth opened under his, how her breasts filled his hands, how her thighs softened for him as he discovered her tender flesh.

He shifted uneasily at his arousal, cautious after the doctor's warning. But the doctor hadn't told him to avoid sex—just bread, pasta and sweets. He'd rather have sex than spaghetti, anyway. And the doctor told him to take a vacation. Giorgio remembered how Renata had talked about her ancestral homeland—Cinque Terre—the Five Lands, a beautiful curve of beach on the Italian Riviera. Relatively quiet this time of year and perfect for a holiday. A holiday for two? She had wanted him as much as he wanted her.

Before he could second-guess the wisdom of inviting a woman he barely knew to visit Europe with him, he found her number on his phone and pressed Send. For once, he would put his own needs before his country's. He would put aside his princely duties this once, and instead just be a man pleasing a woman.

RENATA FUMBLED FOR HER ringing phone and managed to answer it. She'd just fallen asleep after mentally reliving her tumultuous day.

"Renata? It's Giorgio."

"Giorgio?" She yawned. "Are you okay?"

"No."

She sat up in bed, alarmed at the roughness of his voice. "What's wrong? Do you need help?"

"I need you."

"Oh." She looked at the clock. A 4:00 a.m. booty call was not something she'd ever answered. "It's very late and I have to go to work soon." How disappointing he would pull a stunt like this.

"No, not now, I realize that." He exhaled harshly. "I am making an ass of myself. Let me try again. Renata, I can't stop thinking about you. Ever since I dropped you off, all I see is the smile on your face, your hair falling around your shoulders, the scent of you, the taste of your skin…"

She gulped. If this was a booty call, it was a very poetic and arousing one. Maybe she should reconsider her policy…

But he was continuing. "I do need you. I want to know you better, know what you think about things, what you like to read, see at the movies, do for fun. And I want to show you your family's ancestral village on the coast. Come with me to Italy."

Renata patted herself on the cheek to make sure she was really awake having this conversation and not just a really weird dream. If it was a dream about Giorgio, wouldn't she come up with something a little more erotic like actually having sex with the man instead of receiving odd phone calls inviting her to Europe?

"Renata? Will you come?"

Oh, yes, she was awake after all and therefore had to decide what to do. "But, my business—"

"Your assistant you mentioned or your artist friend Flick can manage, can't they? I will pay for a temp if you need one. You have a passport?"

"Yes, I suppose they could manage for a few days."

"A week?"

Her eyebrows shot up. "A week? And I have a passport." She'd gone to Montreal for a short vacation last year. Enough of this beating around the bush. "But, Giorgio, why me? We just met this—well, yesterday morning. Why should I upend my life and take off to Italy with you like some royalty groupie?"

"You know why." His voice deepened to a seductive growl. "Because you *want* me. Me, the man, not the prince. You want what I can give you, but not at the boutique or the jewelry store. You want what I can give you in the bedroom."

Oh, he had her there. The man wasn't even in the same borough with her and was making her crazy for him.

"Remember how I sucked on your nipples last night?

Remember how I touched your silky thighs and hot, sweet center?"

She let out a moan in remembrance.

"That was just a taste of how it could be." Triumph tinged his voice. "I may be a prince in public, but I would be your slave in the bedroom."

A whimper escaped her lips. With talk like that, he could take her to bed anywhere and she'd be more than happy. "Yes."

"Wonderful. I will make arrangements and send them to you tomorrow."

"This morning," she corrected.

He gave a startled laugh. "I'm sorry I hadn't waited until a reasonable time to call you."

"That's fine with me," she reassured him. He'd promised to be her sex slave and she was going to hold him to it.

"Good." His voice dropped into the purr again. "Now think of all the things you want to see in Italy and I will do my utmost to fulfill your wishes."

Number one—see his naked body. Number two—see the bedroom ceiling. Number three—see the bed's headboard. Well, she could maybe come up with some tourist activities. Or not.

"Good night, Giorgio."

"*Ciao, bella* Renata. My only thoughts are of you until I see you again."

She waited until she'd hung up to whimper again. She had a feeling she was going to be just as much a sex slave as he was. Did she mind?

She gave a very New York shrug in the darkness of her bedroom. Nah, of course not.

"So a real-life sexy prince wants to whisk you off to Italy, have his royal wicked way with you and you are hesitating *why?*" The next morning, Flick put her hands on her hips and blew a long turquoise hunk of hair out of her eyes, spoiling the punk persona she cultivated. She wore ripped-up jeans, a holey lime-green T-shirt and safety pins decorating both. A black military surplus jacket and black combat boots with chrome hardware-store chain strung around like tinsel made her look like a scary Christmas tree.

"I'm not that kind of girl," Renata replied virtuously, crossing her legs primly on her elevated desk chair. She made a face at Flick's raucous laughter. "Oh, knock it off. I'm not that kind of girl *anymore.*"

Her friend snorted. "That's only because it's been years since you've had a decent opportunity to be 'that kind of girl.' What's with the cold feet?"

"Oh, all right," she said tersely. "Let's say I do go. What do I tell my aunt?"

"Tell her the truth—you're going on an extended European hookup with one of the tabloids' most eligible bachelors."

"Eeeww, is he really on that list?" Not that Renata wanted Giorgio to have a wife and four kids, but holy crap, was that cheesy.

"Hand to God." Flick cleared a stack of files onto the floor and flopped in the small chair across from Renata's drawing table. "After you called me to come over, I looked him up on my phone. 'Prince Giorgio Armani Ferragamo Versace Gucci Pucci is the crown prince of Vinciguerra—'"

"That is not his name," Renata interrupted.

Flick gave her a sly look. "What is his full name, Miss How-Do-You-Say-Torrid-Vacation-Fling-In-Italian?"

Renata pursed her lips. "Giorgio di Leone. And no, I don't know his middle name."

"Middle names, plural. He has about five. But you only have to know the first. 'Oh, yes, Giorgio. Oh, just like that,

Giorgio.' Et cetera." She ducked out of the way as Renata flung a fat illustration marker at her head, having uttered those very words last night in his limo. "Don't waste your energy on me—save it for Prince Loverboy."

Deciding she didn't want to pay for a replacement desk lamp if it broke when she hurled it at Flick, Renata restrained herself. "Speaking of names, *Felicity,* you really are annoying sometimes. I thought your name meant happiness and joy."

Flick, who had the hide of an elephant, blew her a kiss. "I'm the annoyance who's going to watch your shop while you go happily and joyfully off to Italy. And if you promise me a nice souvenir, I'll even lie to your aunt so she doesn't find out how sex-crazed you really are."

Renata repressed a shudder. If her aunt found out, that meant her whole family found out. "Just what would you tell her?"

"What does your aunt want to sew more than anything?"

"Big poufy dresses," she replied promptly.

"Exactly. So you are going to Europe on a buying trip for lace, ribbons, beads—"

"Sequins and pearls." Renata got the picture. "But I don't want to shop for all that stuff."

"Dumbass, what do princes have secretaries for? Tell the man you need to take some Italian fabric and notions samples home and he will get his staff to pull together a nice portfolio while you romance the hours away."

"Hmm." She tapped her teeth with an unflung marker. "And what do I do when Aunt Barbara asks me about actually making a dress with that? I won't use most of it."

"Have that geeky cousin of yours set up a website for her. She can advertise traditional Italian-American wedding gowns and call it Gowns of Amore or something."

"Not bad, Flick. You put the 'genius' in 'evil genius.'"

"I aim to please. Now if I'm going to be babysitting your biz for the next ten days, you need to get me up to speed."

Renata emailed Flick's phone a copy of her schedule. "Open the file and I'll go over it with you."

"Fine, but don't forget that souvenir you promised me. No airport gift shop crap—you'll have to drag yourself out of the boudoir and actually buy me something nice."

"Sorry, I don't think an Italian gigolo would fit in my suitcase."

"I think your prince Giorgio would be able to make arrangements. Young, hot and stupid are my top requirements."

Renata had to laugh. "I love you, Flick."

Her friend made a noise like a cat with a hair ball. "My God, the prospect of illicit nooky is making you absolutely maudlin. Put a sock in it and tell me about your crowd of Bridezillas. And don't think I won't text you if they give me any crap—loverboy or not."

"I still love you, anyway."

"Arrgh! Get laid already, will you?"

6

AND THAT WAS HOW Renata Pavoni of Brooklyn, New York, U.S.A., found herself ensconced in a first-class seat on Air Italia flying in to Genoa, Italy. Christopher Columbus's hometown and the start of her own adventure. From what she'd read online Genoa was still a busy port town, the biggest city on the Italian Riviera. The coastline of the Riviera curved in a half-moon along the blue Ligurian Sea, stretching from France in the east almost two hundred miles to Tuscany on the west.

The plane touched down with barely a blip and Renata stared out at the early-morning skies, the ugly industrial views of the Genovese airport looking like any other modern airport.

Giorgio's driver-bodyguard, Paolo, stood at the gate as planned. *"Buona sera, signorina."* He relieved her of her carry-on bag. After claiming her luggage, he hustled her to a nondescript beige sedan.

So Giorgio didn't even come along for the ride to the airport. Hmmph. She slid in the back and Paolo got in the driver's seat, accelerating out of the lot as if he were in a Ferrari Testarossa. How much English did this guy speak, anyway? She decided to try out her American Italian. *"Dov'è il principe?"* Just where the hell was that prince?

"Ah, *nell'albergo.* The hotel," he pronounced carefully, the *h* sound foreign to the Italian language. "He wait for you there. At the airport, sometimes paparazzi. Photos." He made noises like the clicking of a camera.

Oh-kay. Needless to say, Renata had never dated anyone who would have been even remotely interesting to a paparazzo photographer. She did hope they'd be able to go out in public without too much obnoxiousness.

Paolo silently drove through the city to a dock at the waterfront. "We need to take boat. No road to Vernazza—the village where we stay in Cinque Terre. Trains not here until morning."

"Oh, okay." Maybe they would have some privacy there if it was only accessible by boat and train.

He carried her luggage down to a medium-size cabin cruiser and nodded to the captain with curly salt-and-pepper hair and a navy blue short-sleeved shirt. After settling her in a lounge-type room, he disappeared upstairs to the bridge. Renata spotted a mini fridge and liberated a water bottle. Flick had warned her about dehydration on long flights and Renata wanted to be dewy-skinned and bright-eyed when she met Giorgio again.

After slugging back a full bottle, she stretched out on the long sofa and covered herself with her travel wrap, a giant pashmina-lookalike shawl she'd spotted at a Brooklyn resale shop. Get the sleep stuff out of the way so they could move directly to the bed part.

It felt as if she had just dozed off when she heard Paolo's voice rumble through the salon. "Signorina Renata? We are here." They had stopped at another dock. Paolo helped her off the boat. "Only a little more." He took off up the hill past several square-looking buildings fastened somehow into a very steep cliff. Well, they hadn't fallen into the sea yet. Glad she had worn sensible shoes for once, Renata followed him to a three-story house a few blocks from the ocean. Paolo showed her a narrow set of stone steps leading to a dark wooden door. "Up the steps, *signorina*."

Renata gripped the handrail as she climbed the stairs. Butterflies hatched in her stomach. What if things had changed between them since their last meeting? Did he still feel the same heat, the same longing she'd fought to keep in check?

Giorgio appeared at the top. She climbed faster but he couldn't wait and clattered down to meet her. "Renata *mia*." *My Renata.*

He pulled her into his arms and firmly dispelled her worries with his kiss. Her neck was cricked up and the handrail poked her in the butt, but who cared? She grabbed his nape and ground her mouth into his. She eagerly accepted his tongue and sucked him deep.

He groaned and dragged her up the rest of the stairs, kicking the door shut behind him. She kept her mouth locked on his and dropped her purse and tote bag on the floor. His shirt was the next to fall as she shoved it off his shoulders, followed by her cropped travel cardigan and wrinkle-resistant linen-look blouse.

Giorgio paused for a second to gaze reverently at her breasts, this time wearing a white satin bra trimmed with matching lace. He didn't say anything, but his eyes darkened to jade and his pupils dilated. As if breaking a trance, he leaped back into action and fumbled with the snap to her capri pants, stripping them down her legs in such haste he took her bikini panties with them—no thongs for her on an eleven-hour flight, complete with plane change in Rome.

She kicked off her white sandals and freed her legs until she stood before him in nothing but her bra. Giorgio scooped her up and carried her through a small living room down the narrow hallway leading to a medium-size bedroom. The dark wooden four-poster bed dominated the room, but there was space for a small table and a floral-upholstered chaise longue.

The matching floral bedspread was pulled back, showing snowy-white linens. He set her carefully on the cushiony mattress and stood back. She rested on her elbows, her ankles crossed. His eyes were hungry, his breathing quick.

"Renata, tu sei la donna più bella del mondo."

That was a promising start. Being called the most beautiful woman in the world was always a plus. Not that she'd ever been called that before, especially in Giorgio's lustfully raspy Italian voice, so different than his normally smooth tones.

"Grazie." She sat up and unfastened her bra, letting her heavy breasts dangle freely.

Her complete nudity was too much for him and his pants and bikini briefs hit the floor. So did her jaw.

Giorgio was regally built in every sense of the word. No wonder his ancestors had held power for several hundred years, being fruitful and multiplying successive generations of princes.

He grinned at her, his physique perfect in the morning light. His broad chest was dusted with black hair that narrowed into a sexy trail down his flat belly, widening into a thick patch showcasing his impressive royal assets.

"That's right—I forgot we did not get this far in the confines of the limo. But now I have plenty of time to make it up to you."

"Please do." His cock was long and thick, toasty brown with a plump head. He knelt next to her on the bed and she couldn't help herself, wrapping her hand around his shaft. He had lovely smooth skin, hot and soft over a core of steel.

She moved up and down and he groaned, tossing his head back. A silvery sheen seeped from the tip, and she spread the moisture around with her thumb.

He grabbed her wrist as if to stop her but she cupped his heavy sac with her other hand and he hissed out a sharp breath. "Renata," he moaned, his hips jerking into her caresses.

"Giorgio," she replied, an answering warmth between her thighs.

"Stop." His hand closed over hers. "I have been dreaming about you for days, waking up like this. Give me a second to regain some control so I can properly make love to you."

"This seems pretty proper to me." She moved underneath him and let her knees fall open. "You're not the only one with hot, nasty dreams, Giorgio."

He shuddered with desire and quickly protected himself. No little illegitimate princes running around for them.

"Are you sure?" He moved between her legs and stared down at her, his green eyes hot but tender.

She hooked her ankles around his calves. "Absolutely."

He glided into her as if they had been lovers for a thousand years, locking himself to her. She gasped at the feel of him—hot and thick, stretching her very core. She couldn't help squeezing down on him and he jerked inside her. "Ah, Renata." He began moving, almost against his will.

She arched her back and raised her hips at him. If she thought the full heft of his cock was heavenly standing still, his thrusting was amazing. Lovely pressure alternating with a sense of emptiness. She wrapped her legs around his waist, pulling him close.

He buried his face in her neck, kissing the tender skin and murmuring to her in raw, raunchy Italian exactly how she made him feel and how he was going to make her come like she'd never come before.

Giorgio had that part right, especially when he reached between their legs and thumbed her clit. She dug her short, red nails into his shoulders and nearly bucked him off her.

He lowered more of his weight to settle on her, pinning her firmly to the bed. She was going nuts, gasping and writhing under him as his skilled fingers plucked at her as if she were a fine musical instrument. His body clung and pulled at her, his lovely olive skin glistening with sweat.

Heat roiled up from where they joined, making her shake and burn. "Giorgio." She gasped out his name, not wanting to climax so quickly.

"*Si, cara mia.* Let yourself go," he coaxed. "Let me take you where you long to be." He hooked her legs over his shoulders and rose up on his knees. He was deep and hard, his hands free to caress her breasts and clitoris.

"Ahh…" She couldn't help moaning as he pinched her nipples, stroked her clit, all the while pounding into her. It was brash and wild, his domination of her. She couldn't move her hips back up at him, and to her surprise, she loved it.

His lips curved into a knowing smile. "You like this, don't you? Oh, wicked, wicked Renata."

She shook her head, not in denial but in her rising passion. Giorgio was relentless, plundering her body. She sucked in a deep breath as the exquisite pleasure built and shattered her, up from her belly into her breasts and out her mouth in a loud scream of ecstasy. Make that several loud screams of ecstasy. If anyone had wondered what the new guests at the villa were up to, she had thoroughly dispelled any false impressions.

He left her weak and trembling under him as he slowed his pace, lowering her legs to the bed. "More?"

She shook her head. She was absolutely wrung out. "I can't even think."

"Good. Just feel." And there he went again, bending to her breasts as he took her again. His slick mouth sucked and nipped at her breasts, coaxing the throbbing peaks to a rosy pink.

Believe it or not, she wasn't done. This time she could move her hips and she did with a vengeance, rising up to meet his driving thrusts. He tossed his head back, a matching groan escaping from him. She reached up and fastened her mouth on his shoulder, salty and slick under her tongue.

"I'll do that to your cock next time," she promised, tremors building again.

He flinched and jerked inside her, hitting her G-spot. She dug her heels into the mattress and her fingers into his ass. "Do it, now!" She felt her control slipping away and disintegrated into a screaming mass of nerves. He let out a shout and followed her, his neck pulling into cords as every muscle in his body tensed.

Giorgio's climax was as long and impressive as he was. She held tight to him, kissing the slick skin of his chest and shoulders wherever she could reach. He finally stopped and smiled down at her, sweat making little black curls at his temples and the nape of his neck. "Give me a second to start breathing again."

"You can have two."

He laughed and kissed her, his body sliding over hers. They were both sticky and wet, and her hair had to be a fright, but who cared?

After a quick bathroom detour, he collapsed at her side, still gasping for air. She went up on one elbow and looked down at him. "Wow."

He grinned at her. "Yes, as you say, 'wow.'" He pulled her down for a quick kiss.

She rolled onto her back. "I mean, geez, I knew it would be something but that was *something*."

It was his turn to lean over her. "I knew we would be like this together. I had to hide my desire for you with a suit jacket in the first minutes we met."

"Really?" Smooth, suave Giorgio had had an unexpected hard-on for the dress designer? "I'm flattered."

"No, I am flattered that you would be here with me. So beautiful." He ran a tender hand over her cheek, her breasts and hips. "Give me a little while and I will show you how flattered I am."

She smiled and touched his face. "We won't let that one go to waste."

He kissed her hand and pulled her into a spooning position. Even soft, his cock was impressive against her bottom. She wiggled experimentally and he groaned. "Insatiable woman. I can see I will have my hands full with you." To emphasize his words, he cupped her breast in his hand.

She giggled. "Your hands, your mouth, your cock…" She giggled again as he snorted in surprise. "What? Do I shock you?"

"Only in the best way possible. I had forgotten how blunt New Yorkers can be."

The New Yorker yawned. "It's been about sixteen hours since I left there, but I am perfectly willing to boss you around in bed once I get my second wind."

"You say that, but I knew what you wanted." He tongued her earlobe and she shivered. He lowered his voice to a honey-eyed purr. "You loved it when I pinned you down—your sweet little pussy tightened even more on me. Your body will tell me what you want."

She swallowed hard. Dammit, he was right. She yawned elaborately again and he immediately pulled a soft cotton sheet over their naked forms. "Rest, *mia bella*. I do not want to wear you out the first day."

His breathing quickly fell into the slow, regular pattern

of sleep, but to her annoyance, she was still awake and thinking about what he had said. Yes, he had possessed her in the most elemental sense of the world, pinned her down and taken her like the lord of the manor and the local lovely virgin peasant girl.

On the other hand, the lord of the manor wouldn't have bothered to make the peasant girl come screaming twice in five minutes.

Renata was a modern girl, used to taking charge in her life and in the bedroom, as well, if need be. But what if she didn't need to take charge? It was an interesting idea. Not that she wanted to bring out any weird leather accoutrements that were ho-hum among certain friends of Flick's, but if she were going to do the deed with an honest-to-goodness prince, she may as well try new things. The man was born and bred to be bossy.

And if she wanted some turnabout…she smiled in satisfaction, remembering how he'd crumbled like a cracker when she'd grabbed his erection. A well-placed hand—or mouth—and he'd be putty in her hands. Well, not really putty—she wanted him firmer than that.

7

THE NEXT MORNING, GIORGIO stood on the apartment's terrace and gazed at the bright blue sea dotted with white sails. A fresh breeze ruffled his hair, and he couldn't stop grinning. So much so, his face was starting to hurt.

So this was what freedom felt like. Freedom to wear a battered football shirt—not that Dieter's team, of course—and battered cargo shorts and just stare at the water. Freedom to spend time with a wonderful woman without prying eyes wondering who she was, how long they had been dating and whether or not she would be the next Princess of Vinciguerra.

He didn't have to worry about weddings, deepwater port negotiations or the price of coffee in Vinciguerra. Alessandro was ably manning the fortress and had been providing daily email briefs with strict instructions to call only if absolutely necessary. Even Paolo'd made himself scarce.

He slipped on a pair of sandals, a baseball hat and sunglasses. Once he hid his distinctive green eyes, he pretty much looked like any other young Italian man going to buy coffee and rolls for his sleeping girlfriend.

The café down the street was narrow but fragrant with the scents of coffee beans, cream, vanilla and sugar. He purposely put on a thick Roman accent when ordering, just in case the counter girl enjoyed flipping through *People* magazine. World's Most Eligible Bachelor, pah! Jack and Frank had busted a gut laughing, as the Americans said, and he wouldn't have put it past his sister to have been the person who nominated him. They had had a tiff last winter when she had wanted to drop out of grad school to follow Jack's merry men of medicine to Ulaan Baator or Timbuktu or Bora Bora.

Fortunately Jack had declined her offer since a background in international politics was of little use in treating infections and parasites. Although several international politicians he'd met somehow brought parasites and infection to mind.

He accepted the caffe lattes and pastries with a smile of anticipation at waking Renata. She'd roll over in bed, smile sweetly up at him—maybe even beckon him to her as the coffee grew cold and the pastries grew stale. Yes, a sweet morning wake-up for both of them.

RENATA SQUINTED AS A BAND of dreaded sunlight crossed her eyelids. She wrapped the sheet tighter around her naked body. After their long, exciting night she hadn't bothered pulling on a sexy negligee or cotton T-shirt, her normal sleepwear.

"Rise and shine, Sleeping Beauty," a husky male voice crooned. "I know you have jet lag but it's almost ten o'clock. Come get some sun and you'll feel better."

"No, I won't." Renata rolled onto her stomach and buried her head under a pillow.

"I have coffee, *cara mia*," Giorgio coaxed. "Lots of cream and sugar and fresh pastries. Just the thing to wake you up."

She pried open a gritty eye to stare at him. He sounded

entirely too perky for her liking. But she did like how the thin soccer T-shirt outlined his chest muscles nicely and his shorts showed strong brown legs. He obviously got more exercise than pushing a pencil across his desk and cracking the whip over peasants. "Giorgio, it's five o'clock in the morning New York time and I'm achy from that long flight."

"Okay, Renata." He set the tray onto the dresser and crossed the room. "Let me loosen you up."

The mattress dipped as he moved onto the bed next to her. Warm hands moved over her shoulders, massaging and loosening them. She sighed as he found all the knotted muscles. "Where'd you learn to do that?"

"I took classes as a massage therapist in case the prince thing didn't work out for me."

A snort escaped her.

"What? You don't believe me? Europe can be a very volatile place and it is always good to have a backup plan."

With that sexy five o'clock shadow, his backup plan ought to be a new career as a male underwear model. Somehow she doubted the massage school. "What's your degree in?"

"International finance. If you ever have trouble sleeping some night, I will tell you all about the Mundell-Fleming model, the optimal currency area theory and the purchasing power parity theory."

It made her yawn just to hear their names. "Good Lord, are those for real?"

He leaned forward and whispered in her ear, "The purchasing power parity theory originated in Spain in the sixteenth century and was modernized by Gustav Cassel in the early twentieth."

"Oh, don't stop, don't stop," she teased him. "Keep talking finance to me, Giorgio."

He laughed. "Will emerging market economies ever become decoupled from developed market economies?"

"Oooh, coupling. Now that sounds kinky."

He brushed her hair to the side and rubbed her neck. "Glad to hear that. There are many more theories where those came from."

He pulled the sheet away and did long strokes down her back to her ass, kneading each cheek with strong hands. She gasped as wetness grew between her thighs. "Oh, so tense here. You will need plenty of massage to loosen such a delicate area."

Somehow his massage had passed from therapeutic to intimate when he stopped massaging and bent to kiss his handiwork. He murmured in between kisses. She squirmed against his mouth. "Soft and round. I have wanted to do this since I saw you walking away from me in that tight black skirt. I almost drooled right there."

Oh, yes, Giorgio liked traditional Italian butts.

He circled his tongue around the base of her spine and rubbed his cheek across, well, *her* cheek. The stubble prickled her skin and she pushed her hips into the bed, futilely trying to ease the ache.

She looked to see why he had stopped and saw him pulling his clothes off and popping on a condom. Sunlight played across his naked body, with nary a flaw to be seen. If he hadn't literally drooled all over her butt just now, she'd have quite the inferiority complex.

He urged her onto her hands and knees. "Oh, yes," she breathed as he knelt behind her, his tip brushing her as he nudged her knees wider.

"Open for me, lovely Renata." He circled her clit with his finger, spreading her folds wide. He slid back and forth between them, his head nudging her clit with every stroke. But she still ached inside for him to fill her.

She arched her back, tipping up for him. He accepted her invitation as he slid inside with a single deep thrust.

She screamed in shocked satisfaction. "Yes, Giorgio, ohh…"

He grunted and kept pushing in and out of her. No more pretty words from him. Her butt ground against his flat belly, his balls swinging into her. His fingers dug into her hips as he pounded her. She clutched the headboard for support and he cupped her breasts with his big hands. She shuddered and tightened on him.

"Ah, Renata, *si,* that's it." He was relentless in his ravishing, the headboard knocking the wall with his thrusts. Her hair stuck to the nape of her neck as he sucked on her earlobe. She started to shake and gasp, wanting to pull away from his intensity but loving it at the same time.

He reached between her thighs to massage her hard, swollen clit and that was it for her. She arched backward, resting her head on his shoulder as he ruthlessly dragged her to amazing peaks of pleasure. His arm tightened over her breasts and he nipped at her neck while she screamed his name. He followed her over the edge, coming so hard she thought they'd break the bed.

He moaned in her ear, and she twisted to look at him and he captured her mouth with his, plunging his tongue deep between her lips, mimicking his cock below. He gave one last shudder and wrenched his mouth from hers, gasping for air. "Ah…*Dio mio,* Renata."

She dropped her head, amazed at the explosive, raunchy sex. A couple minutes of massage foreplay, a couple minutes of thrusting and she was purring like a kitten.

He eased from her and she gladly collapsed back onto the mattress, covering her eyes with her arm.

"Renata?" he asked cautiously, easing down next to her. "Are you all right?"

She stared up at him. "I want you to be honest with me, Giorgio."

"Yes?" He raised a black eyebrow.

"I know this is a personal question, but we're getting pretty personal here so I'll ask anyway. Is sex always like this with you?"

He made kind of a choking noise but didn't say anything.

She continued, "I mean, I figured you and I would be hot together after that limo incident, and you've got the biggest, best cock I've ever seen, but this—" she gestured to their naked, sweaty, sticky bodies "—this is past hot. It's positively nuclear."

"Nuclear," he echoed. "And you say I have the biggest—" Words failed him again.

"Biggest, best, hottest, thickest cock I or any other woman in New York has ever seen. And before Parsons, I went to art school where we drew lots of naked men, so I've seen a bunch."

"And you say I have the best?" He had gotten over his shock and his masculine pride was kicking in, a proud smile spreading over his face.

"Oh, please. Surely some woman already told you that."

"Not in such detail. And since you want me to be honest, I have never been…nuclear…like this with any other woman."

"Oh, come on," she scoffed. "You've probably dated some of the most beautiful women in the world."

He paused for a second, as if to think back. "I've been photographed with many beautiful women. I've kissed some of them, but there's a big difference between publicity and reality. None of them have the same spark, the same joy of living that you bring to everything you do."

"Everything?" His words thrilled her as much as his body did.

"Oh, definitely. Designing dresses, eating chili dogs, making love to me…"

He rolled her against him so they were breast-to-chest, belly-to-belly and nuclear parts-to-nuclear parts. Even after detonation, his rocket was still in launch position. "I can only give you all the credit. You, with your beautiful ivory face and thick red hair like a beautiful Renaissance painting by Titian. And your ripe, lush body." He skimmed his hand over her curves. "You have a body made for pleasure. And I am incredibly flattered you would share it with me. There has not been any woman like you before." He kissed her again, this time softly and sweetly.

"Wow," she said weakly after the kiss had ended. "Do they teach you all that poetic stuff in prince school?"

"No, I find that you are quite the inspiration." He kissed the tip of her nose and pushed up out of bed. "Stay there. Our coffee may still be warm." He grabbed his clothes and hurried into the bathroom. Renata wrapped the sheets around her again. No sense in tempting fate with nudity and hot coffee.

He quickly reappeared in the same casual outfit and brought the tray over to the bed. *"Un caffe latte per la Signorina."* He carefully took the lid off the to-go cup and she sipped at the coffee.

"Yep, you're right—still warm."

"And a fresh almond pastry." He handed her a soft square sprinkled with toasted almonds and drizzled with white sugar glazing.

"Mmm, delicious." Crumbs flaked off the pastry. "Look, I'm making a mess of the bed."

Giorgio grinned, and Renata took a good look at the bed. Pastry crumbs were the least of it. One pillow was in the hallway, the top sheet was wrapped around her like a toga, and the bottom sheet had been totally wrenched free by their frantic couplings. Even the headboard stood in danger of bashing a hole in the wall. Short of dumping the coffee over the bedding, it was a total wreck.

He cleared his throat delicately. "Did I mention maid service comes with the villa rental?"

"Good thing." She raised her cup in a toast and they ate a surprisingly companionable breakfast among the cheerful mess. Giorgio was turning out to be lots of fun, and not just in bed. This was going to be a great vacation.

And after? The unwelcome thought popped up. Well, Giorgio would need to come to New York sometime, and maybe she would see him then. A friends-with-benefits thing?

Renata must have grimaced because Giorgio asked if she wanted more sugar in her coffee.

She decided to enjoy the moment and stop worrying about the future. "No, it's perfect. Everything is just perfect."

RENATA SMILED AT HER reflection in the compact bathroom. Although it had obviously been added after the original construction of the ancient house, it managed to hold all the necessities, plus the ubiquitous European bidet. She stared down at that white porcelain fixture. She'd never tried one before and the sunny Italian Riviera would freeze over before she asked Giorgio how to use it.

Bidets aside, the shower had actually had pretty good water pressure, which was necessary to repair the red wreckage of her hair. She ran a brush through her hair and pulled it into a twist, fastening it with a black lacquer clip.

She slipped on a V-neck sapphire silk blouse and a black circle skirt that poufed around her knees thanks to a hidden tulle crinoline. Both were amazingly wrinkle-free despite how she'd seen the baggage handlers treat her luggage.

A matching small sapphire stud went into the side of her

nose. She owned an assortment of different studs except for ruby—no sense in looking like she had an acne breakout. Red lips to match her nails completed the look, and she smacked them to set the color. Dressy, but casual enough for a seaside dinner at a local restaurant.

She stopped briefly to grab her pashmina wrap out of the closet, not sure how cool the breeze became, and then swanned out of the bedroom into the living room.

Giorgio was standing in front of one of the tall, narrow windows that lined the living room at the front of the apartment. The sun had set a few minutes ago, and twilight illuminated his profile as he looked out over the sea. His strong but straight nose, his full lips and determined chin. He was so beautiful she felt a painful thump in her chest. But he was hers, at least for now.

Giorgio turned as she approached. Hopefully the dim light hid her face as she mooned over him. "There you are, Renata." He flipped on a small table lamp and brought her back to reality.

Reaching for her hand, he inspected her from head to toe. "I didn't want to hurry you, and I see that my wait has been more than worthwhile. You are as lovely as always."

"Thank you." She returned the inspection. "You look great, too." He wore a short-sleeved black silk button-down shirt over loose linen trousers and leather sandals, a summer uniform for many European men, but he made it look like the cover of Italian *GQ*.

"I'm glad you approve." He said it seriously, as if there were some miniscule chance in this universe that she wouldn't. Short of donning a seventies' leisure suit and fifteen gold chains, Giorgio could never look bad. And even then, the clothing's ugliness would just highlight his good looks.

"Who picks out your clothes?" she asked.

"My clothes?" He looked confused and then glanced at his pants and shirt.

"Yeah, do you go shopping, or do they bring items for you to try?"

"I have a personal shopped in Rome," he admitted, as if it were a deep, shameful secret. "Unfortunately I don't have much time for shopping but have many outings and functions to attend, so Antonio has my measurements and brings me new outfits every month or so."

Renata whistled under her breath. That would be a cool gig for a menswear salesman. "He does a nice job," she reassured him. "You look very distinguished." She had another thought. "So when we go out for dinner, do we need to do a perp walk?"

"A what?"

She pulled her pashmina over her head to hide her face. "When the FBI arrests gangsters, they always pull their suit jackets over their head and scuttle by the reporters on the way back to the jail. Of course it's not like there aren't a million pictures of them floating around there anyway." She popped her head free and patted her hair.

He was staring at her in amazement.

"Seriously, you lived in New York for all of your college years and you never heard of the perp walk?"

He nodded. "Must have missed it."

"Another trick is to drape your jacket over your wrists so it hides the handcuffs. But who carries their suit coat that way? Who do they think they're fooling?"

"Not you, obviously."

"Not me. Two of my brothers are cops and two are firefighters. They know all the good dirt."

"I see."

Well, maybe he did. But he'd probably lived in a swanky flat on the Upper East Side, a world away from mobsters in federal court. And a world away from Renata, her four brothers and two parents sandwiched into a Brooklyn bungalow.

"No, Renata, we don't need to do a perp walk to go out in public. I've never been here before and have managed to keep my face out of most of the tabloids."

"Except for *People* magazine's most eligible bachelor list," she needled him.

The pained expression on his face was priceless. "If I ever meet who nominated me for that damned list I will have very harsh words for them. Stefania made me autograph several dozen copies of the magazine so she could auction them for her charity. And then she wanted to sell *me* for charity in a bachelor auction."

"A bachelor auction?"

He winced again. "Yeah, that—like a gigolo hanging around a bar."

"That reminds me—Flick wants you to send her an Italian gigolo. Young, hot and stupid."

He choked with laughter. "Let me call my assistant and have him start looking."

"If he's handsome, just send him instead. I'm sure Flick would give him a good time."

"You New York girls are too bold—I think she would frighten poor Alessandro."

Renata walked over to the floral-print couch that could have been in any working-class Brooklyn living room and posed herself. "And are you frightened of this New York girl, poor little Giorgio?" Honey was sour compared to her voice. "Little Giorgio" was looking not frightened at all, instead rather pleased as it tried to escape his linen trousers.

"As always, I live to serve." He watched avidly as she slowly drew her hemline upward, revealing the sheer black stockings and matching garters he'd loved the first day they met.

"Good," she purred, beckoning him with one red-tipped finger. "Serve *me*."

8

MUCH LATER THAN THEY had planned, Giorgio and Renata sat down to dinner. "See? Dinner out and no perp walk necessary." Giorgio gestured to the busy restaurant. It was obviously a family place with the waiters and waitresses wearing T-shirts decorated with sports team logos. Most of the tables were lined up in rows almost cafeteria style, but Giorgio had finagled himself a table set apart on the corner of the stone terrace. They sipped a fantastic white wine as they sat overlooking the ocean.

"Someday I'll see what this place looks like in daylight." It was fantastic anyway at night, the sky purple against the Ligurian Sea while an ivory pillar candle flickered on the table. Soft Italian pop music played in the background, dimming the clink of silverware and cheerful conversations nearby.

"And whose fault is that? If it weren't for the land-lady stocking the kitchen before we arrived, I would have starved for food." He rubbed his thumb across the back of her hand. "But not starved for you, Renata *mia*. I think you have taken care of that for now."

She gave him a goofy grin and he smiled back at her.

"The candlelight becomes you, Renata. Fiery to match your hair—and your passion."

"Shh." She pressed her finger against his mouth. "This isn't exactly a fortress of solitude, you know."

"Fiery to match your blush." He smooched her finger.

"Must be the reflection." Her cheeks were heating. Wow, she'd thought that autonomic nervous reaction had been permanently deactivated years ago from lack of use. Leave it to Giorgio to trip all sorts of triggers.

"If you say so." A mischievous gleam danced in his eyes. He was really loosening up.

The waiter arrived with a plate of antipasti for them to sample, marinated olives, steamed mussels and fried odds and ends of fresh anchovies and other seafood. Of course there was focaccia—a savory flatbread common to the area—with olive oil for dipping. She pulled a hunk from the bread and swirled it through the oil, dotted with hunks of chopped garlic cloves and minced basil leaves. Totally delish. They couldn't be more than an hour out of the oven. "You should really have some." She held it up to his mouth and he took a small bite.

"Tasty."

"Have some more." She gestured at the large disc. If she ate all that bread herself, her snugly tailored skirts would split down the seams.

He picked up an olive. "Thank you, but I will just enjoy watching you eat."

"You're not on a low-carb diet, are you? I thought that was against the law in Italy."

He shrugged. "I have a taste for these olives tonight. Have you tried the green ones? Very good, and probably grown not too far from here." He dished a few onto her plate, and she had to agree they were very good, especially wrapped up in focaccia.

The waiter set a platter of pasta lavished in rich green pesto sauce in front of them. It had an unusual aroma. The waiter chatted with Giorgio for a minute as he dished up two servings. Giorgio thanked him and they were left alone again.

"He says this pasta is called *trofie* and is made from chestnut flour. The pesto sauce was of course invented in this region and has the typical basil leaf base, mixed with pecorino cheese and pine nuts."

"Don't forget the marjoram." Renata smiled at his look of surprise. "My grandmother taught me how to make pesto. Fortunately we have a food processor now and don't need to grind everything in her old marble mortar and pestle."

"My mamma's specialty was desserts. She was an assistant pastry chef when she met my father. He had an amazing sweet tooth and ordered tiramisu at the hotel where she was working. He asked to meet the chef, and—" he spread his hands wide "—the rest is Vinciguerran history.

Renata's heart tugged at his wistful smile. "What was your favourite dessert she made?"

He looked startled briefly, as if he'd been far away in memory. "Lemon cookies. Lemon bars. Lemon cake."

"Lemon anything." She laughed.

"Oh, yes, especially at the end of a long, gloomy winter. Her lemon cookies were a snap of springtime in my mouth."

Renata wondered if anyone made him lemon cookies anymore. Probably wouldn't be the same if he had to ask. Something so powerful as that was made freely and spontaneously, out of love. Did his grandmother or sister have the recipe? Maybe it wasn't too complicated.

"Hopefully our pesto will live up to your grandmother's high standards." Giorgio offered her a forkful of pasta and she moaned with delight. The nutty flavor of the pasta balanced the tang of the cheese and pine nuts in the pesto. He watched her in satisfaction. "I thought I was the only one who made you sound like that."

She winked. "What can I say? I'm a hedonist at heart."

"You are in the right place." He gestured at the vista in front of them. "Food, wine, song and passion. Even though you were not born here, you belong here. The land and the sea are calling you."

Renata stopped midbite. The land and the sea. Yes, she did feel a connection to this slice of Italy perched between the sea and the mountains. But she thought it was more because of Giorgio's presence. He was the lens through which she had focused so intensely. But she couldn't stay in the Cinque Terre forever.

"And your country, does it call to you?" She hoped so, because he couldn't exactly give two weeks' notice and pack up.

"Yes, but in a different way. I hear the call of my father and my mother, the call of my ancestors who ruled Vinciguerra and fought for her people. I know it's my solemn duty to protect them and make sure they thrive in a modern world while preserving our national heritage."

"That's a big job. No wonder you're so serious." Their main course arrived, a whole fish that had been wandering around in the Ligurian Sea that morning.

Giorgio served them each a portion, the fish flaking enticingly under his fork. "Eh, too serious according to my sister. She thinks I need to lighten up. Be sure to drink your wine with the fish. The waiter says if you drink water with fish, it will start swimming around in your stomach." He grinned at her.

Renata sipped some wine. No reanimated fish for her. "Maybe Stefania should cut you some slack since she's not the one in charge of a country and several thousand people." Renata winced after that. Criticizing his sister was probably a dumb idea. He loved her very much. She stuffed some fish into her mouth to shut herself up. Holy cow, were they all geniuses in the kitchen here or just this restaurant? She'd have to get the recipe for her mother.

But he wasn't offended. "No, you are both correct. I do need to lighten up and yes, I am the one in charge of a country. However, do not let my people hear you say I am in charge of them. They are even more stiff-necked than I am and do not hesitate to point out my errors. I don't know why I ever introduced technology like the internet and email to Vinciguerra." He stopped to dip some fish into the garlicky olive oil and hummed in appreciation.

"Before, they had to buy the newspaper, read it and then either call the palazzo or mail me a letter to complain. Now all they have to do is read electronic news on their phones and immediately text me to tell me what exactly I am doing wrong. I should have left them in the twentieth century." But he was grinning as he said this. "I even had to hire a nineteen-year-old email assistant to decipher the acronyms and lack of vowels. I can tell you I wasn't LOL-ing."

Renata did LOL—laugh out loud. His affection for his country and his subjects—if they even considered themselves as such—was evident. "They boss you around terribly, don't they?"

"It's like I have thousands of nosy but well-meaning aunts and uncles." He raised his wineglass and gestured to the terrace. "Which is why we are here and not in Vinciguerra. No privacy there whatsoever."

"What a pair we are. I have to fly across the Atlantic and you have to sneak out of your country for any time together."

He brushed the corner of her mouth with his thumb. "I would have swum the Mediterranean Sea to be with you."

"How sweet." An unfamiliar wave of mushy sentiment

A **treat** from us to **thank you** for reading our books!

Thanks for reading!

We're treating you to **TWO** fabulous offers...

2 FREE BOOKS

from your favourite Mills & Boon series plus have books delivered to your door every month!

Find out more and claim your free books at
www.millsandboon.co.uk/bookclub

or call 020 8288 2888 and
quote BOOKCLUB today!

Plus **15% OFF** **

Your next order online with code
THANKSMAR at **www.millsandboon.co.uk**

MILLS & BOON

swirled up into her throat as she heard herself practically coo at the man. But she couldn't help it. Large helpings of delicious food, romantic settings and of course hot sex with a capital *H* and a capital *S*.

"How true." He slid his arm around her shoulder. "When I'm with you, you are my only responsibility. I've let my duties deprive me of the normal pleasures of being a man. I'm grateful you reminded me."

Renata played with the fish with her fork. "I've been working like a madwoman for the past several years. I was full-time at the traditional bridal salon and spent evenings and days off designing fun dresses and writing my business plan. I finally opened Peacock Designs two years ago and work even harder than ever."

"We are two of a kind. Driven, ambitious and determined."

"I hate being beholden to anyone," she admitted. "Just so you know, our trip is the first time I've ever accepted anything like this."

He nuzzled her neck. "Renata, Renata, please don't worry. If you were only interested in my money and status, you would have tripled the charges for Stefania's dress, accepted my offer to the hotel immediately and then dragged me to the nearest jeweler for a 'little remembrance' of our time together. And I would have realized what kind of person you were, and extricated myself with a polite excuse."

Jealousy swelled in her stomach and she pointed her fork at him. "Been in that situation before?"

Giorgio kissed her cheek. "Yes, a couple times when I was young and *stupido*. Not in the last several years, of course." His free hand came to rest on her knee, stroking her thigh. "I have become a much better judge of character, but I have never been so impulsive as this."

"Me, neither." She set down her fork. "And since we're being impulsive, why don't we order dessert to go?"

"I impulsively agree." He sat up and signaled the waiter, his hand still on her knee. "Dessert is best eaten in private."

THE NEXT MORNING, Giorgio slipped from their bed and pulled on a pair of shorts. Renata murmured in her sleep and rolled over, a lock of red hair falling over her round white breast to curl around her coral-pink nipple. He nearly changed his mind and slipped back into bed, but realized they had only fallen asleep a few hours earlier and he hated to wake her.

He contented himself with staring at her for a minute, something he couldn't do while she was awake. She reminded him of an Andrew Wyeth painting he had seen at a museum in New York during college—a beautiful redhead sleeping, the sheets falling to her waist to bare her breasts.

Something about the painting had intrigued him, and it wasn't just the sight of a naked woman. The sheer peacefulness of the painting, pale linens, pale skin and a dark window behind, the only color from her hair and the crests of her nipples.

Giorgio realized why he'd been so struck by both the painted woman and Renata, the real woman—it was the sheer trust exhibited to be vulnerable to a man in sleep.

He gazed at her for a minute longer and gave a deep sigh of contentment before walking into the living room. After a quick call, the café across the street was happy to send over a carafe of coffee and platter of pastries. He thought for a second and added an assortment of fruit for him. His doctor had made him promise to eat better. He had wanted Giorgio to stay for more tests and not leave Vinciguerra at all, but once he learned Giorgio was taking a vacation, he stopped protesting.

He tipped the delivery boy and checked on Renata again. She'd rolled onto her back, a round arm slung above her head in sleeping abandon. He couldn't get enough of her, but she'd had enough of him—at least until she woke again.

Some grapes, melon and a small pastry were enough to tide him over and he realized he hadn't checked his phone. Although he almost never turned it off, his time with Renata was an exception. The palazzo had Paolo's number and would notify him if there were a serious problem.

A text from Stefania, inviting him to Germany to have a meet-the-parents dinner with Dieter's family. Lovely, beer and brats for everyone—oh, and maybe sauerkraut and some of those lead ingots that masqueraded as German dumplings. He'd have to check his schedule with Alessandro for the week after his vacation, since hell would freeze over before he cut short his time with Renata.

Mmm, a text from Frank, asking him how New York was and if the German footballer was a suitable match for Stefania. Too complicated to text back.

Frank answered on the second ring. "Hey, George! How's New York?"

"I'm actually back in Italy."

"So quickly? Did they drag you back for the grand opening of an orphanage? Senior citizen center? School for wayward girls?"

"Not exactly," he said cagily.

"Ah," Frank said understandingly. "The Royal Vinciguerran Society for Unwanted Puppies and Kitties?"

Giorgio laughed.

"Ah, you think I'm kidding, but put aside your dislike for animal fur on those expensive suits and think of the possibilities. Prince Giorgio surrounded by frolicking baby animals. Prince Giorgio petting a kitten. Prince Giorgio having his royal face licked by a white fluffy puppy. I tell you, George, the women would fall all over you in a heart-beat."

"Frank, I don't need women falling all over me."

Something in his voice alerted Frank. "Because you already have one?"

Giorgio protested but Frank went charging ahead. "George! You never mentioned this to me when you called about Stevie's engagement. Is it because you didn't want to distract from her news?"

"No, Frank, it's because I didn't know her then."

Well, that got Frank to put a sock in it. But not for long. "My, my, *my!* Aren't you the fast worker. Someone we know?"

"You may meet her—she's designing Stevie's wedding dress."

"So you just met her last Wednesday?"

"Yes," Giorgio muttered.

"So why aren't you back in New York with her? You may have a lot of advantages over us non-princes, but sometimes out of sight means out of mind."

Giorgio rolled his eyes. Francisco Emiliano José Duarte das Aguas Santas was the duke of one of the largest estates in Portugal plus a whole island in the Portuguese Azores and wasn't exactly hurting for female interest. He also happened to know that Frank hadn't always been one to talk about "out of sight, out of mind" when it came to women, one in particular, but that was his business. And Giorgio's business was apparently Frank's business, as well.

"Go back to New York, George. You deserve to have a private life, too."

"You know, I couldn't agree more. That's why I am on the Italian Riviera—and not all by myself."

Another silence—that had to be a record. Then Frank

started to laugh. "You must have swept her off her feet, George. Good job."

"I think she likes me, yes." Giorgio started to wonder how Renata did feel about him, thanks to Frank's line of questioning.

"Obviously, if you convinced her to go to Europe with you after only a few days."

Only a few hours, but that *wasn't* Frank's business.

"Any progress on planning Stevie's wedding?" That would distract Frank for a second.

"Yes, but I asked my mother for some advice and she laughed, George. When I told her one day of a wedding was simple compared to a lifetime of running our estates, she laughed even more."

Giorgio rolled his eyes as Frank continued, "And that was not a nice laugh, George. She told me not to be stupid, that men didn't know anything about weddings except how to get stinking drunk at them."

"We *are* bachelors, Frank."

"Since she wasn't in the mood to be helpful, I ordered a wedding planner notebook from the bookstore and Stevie and I have been emailing back and forth. Her wedding colors will be gold and ivory, and she and Dieter are looking at their calendar to set a date at the Cathedral of Vinciguerra. We'll work on the guest list later."

Wow, Frank needed a different hobby. Or more likely, a woman. Another thought struck him. "About my trip here on the Riviera, Frank…Stevie doesn't know I'm here and doesn't know I'm here with Renata, okay?"

"Renata Pavoni, the dress designer? Stevie emailed me a photo of her dress so I could see the style."

"Right. But keep it quiet, Frank. As far as Stevie knows, I'm back in Vinciguerra."

"Cutting ribbons for dog pounds, right?" Frank laughed

again. "Don't worry, I won't say anything. I told you last week you were burning the candle at both ends, eh? A nice vacation with a pretty girl is just what you need."

"Thank you. Speaking of burning the candle at both ends, have you heard from Jack?" Dr. Jacques needed to write himself a prescription for some R & R.

"He sent me a quick email from his satellite laptop that said he was going upriver and would be incommunicado for a few days. The news service says the flood casualties are even worse than originally reported."

Giorgio shook his head. "He won't be happy until he's come down with some previously unknown dread tropical disease that medical science can name after him." *Jacques stupidii.*

"Or being chased by pirates," Frank agreed. "Talk about a man who needs to relax, huh?"

"If he makes it that long. Especially since we have a wedding to pull off." Not that Jack knew anything about that sort of task, either.

"Right, George. Don't worry about a thing. Stevie and I have it all well in hand, so you enjoy your vacation, okay?"

"And not a word to her about where I am, right?"

"Right. We're just emailing and texting, so she can't tell if I am lying or not." Frank was a terrible liar.

"Good. I'll let you know when I am back in Vinciguerra."

"Take your time—and give that pretty *signorina* a kiss from ol' Frank, okay?"

"Not okay, Frank. Find your own. You should settle down and make little dukes for your mother to spoil."

"Right." His voice was cool for the first time. "What's the American phrase? 'Always the bridesmaid, never the bride.' Well, I am happy to be the wedding planner and never the groom."

Giorgio winced. "Frank—"

"*Tchau,* Giorgio."

"*Ciao,* Franco," he replied, but to an empty line. Ah, he'd touched a nerve there with his offhand comment. As if Giorgio ever talked seriously about settling down. He'd apologize later when Frank had regained his normally sunny mood.

He stared at his phone. Frank was more of a home-body than any of them, preferring to work in the fields or build some new and elaborate project for his estate. Giorgio was the dutiful one, working in the palazzo like some CEO, and Jack had been bitten by the travel bug, probably the least harmful than the rest he'd encountered, and put more stamps in his passport saving the world than the Dalai Lama.

But none of them had had more than short-term relationships that fizzled instead of sizzled. He knew about Frank's unhappy foray into first love only because of a late-night, wine-soaked confession of misery. Giorgio had poured Frank back into his bed that night right before the start of their second year at the university.

Jack had an aloof vibe that drove the girls crazy to learn what was behind the charming, but remote French facade. He'd preferred to go out with the cool, brainy types he met in his premed classes, and once he started medical school, dating fell by the wayside.

And Giorgio had had several girlfriends but had always put Stefania, his grandmother and his country before them—in that exact order. If he'd been his ruthless medieval ancestor, the original Giorgio Martelli di Leone, the Hammer of the Lion, who had carved out a principality from the rugged Italian hills, he would have put country first and women relatives a distant last. He would have sold Stefania off to a husband who offered the most advantage for him, chucked his grandmother in a nunnery if she gave

him any grief and would have married the woman with
the best dowry, regardless of looks or appeal. That original Giorgio had done pretty much the same thing, addi-
tionally fathering roughly a dozen children with nearly as
many women. He'd often met other green-eyed Vinciguerran men who looked enough like him to be a cousin, if not
a brother.

An odd thing, the fortuitous circumstances of his birth.
He'd never thought much about it, traveling through his life
like a swimmer in a river, constantly moving and dealing
with rocks as they popped up. But if his great-something
grandfather had been the son of the dairymaid instead of
the son of the lady of the manor, Giorgio would be another
tall, green-eyed Vinciguerran man reading the morning
paper at his breakfast table and wondering aloud at great
volume what that idiot prince of theirs was up to again.

He sipped his coffee thoughtfully. In that cozy Vinciguerran flat, his beautiful Italian wife, a redhead from
the Cinque Terre, would shrug at the mysteries of foreign-
ers as she poured him a caffe latte and kissed the nape of
his neck.

He brought himself up short. That humble, sweet life that
happened every day in his country was not his life. His flat
was a gigantic palazzo and his life was not conducive to a
normal marriage.

But while he and Renata were here in this lovely town
along a lovely sea, he would make little memories like that
imaginary breakfast and newspaper. And maybe when he
was back at his immense desk arguing over traffic cross-
ings and fishing rights, he would think back to how her
hair curled over her breast as she slept on a sunny spring
morning.

He set his cup down forcefully, awkwardly so the handle
cracked off. Memories. Scraps of life. He was a man who

had almost everything, could get almost anything with the snap of his fingers or the ring of his phone—and he was jealously hoarding mental snapshots to remember like an old widow staring at family photos.

Giorgio jumped to his feet, strangely disconcerted. Who was he to live like this? Had he not been living like this since his parents had died? Remembering how they had been happy and whole, Papa, Mamma, brother and sister. Making Stevie's life happy and whole again seemed to have left a hole in his.

He stalked toward the bedroom. Well, if he was to be a man of memories, he was damn well going to make more.

Slipping off his robe, he slid into bed with Renata. She turned toward him in her sleep, wrapping her soft white arms around him. He swallowed hard and kissed the top of her head. Another memory for Prince Giorgio, rich in worldly goods but a pauper in the things that really mattered.

9

DESPITE HIS BEST EFFORTS to delegate work back to his assistants, Giorgio had to set aside a couple hours to attend to business. Renata did the same but since she was running a shop and not a country, finished sooner. Despite her decidedly antinuptial tendencies, Flick was a smart cookie and had no trouble managing the shop.

Renata closed the app on her phone and went looking for Giorgio. He was sitting on the couch, leaning over a tablet PC while talking to his assistant in rapid Italian. She waited until he paused for breath and then waved to him.

"*Momento,* Alessandro." He pressed mute on the phone. "Renata, sweetheart, I am so sorry. An issue about the new seaport came up. Something about how deep the water must be. I'm in a conference call with our consultants—retired American Naval officers as a matter of fact."

She saluted him and smiled.

"Are you bored? I can have Paolo take you somewhere."

She gestured dismissively. Vernazza wasn't exactly New York, and there she didn't need a bodyguard, either. "I thought I'd take a walk and do some shopping. I need to buy Flick a gift and a little something for my parents and

Aunt Barbara. Maybe a bottle or two of Scciachetrà for a special occasion."

Giorgio peeled several large-denomination euro bills from his clip. "Buy one for us. I can think of several special occasions we can create."

Renata raised an eyebrow. "That's way too much money for a bottle of wine."

"Then buy something for yourself." He pressed the money into her hand. "I know how independent you are, but let me treat you. Something small even."

"Oh, all right." Renata still had mixed feelings about accepting his money but after accepting a whole luxury trip, what was some spending money for wine? He'd drink it, too.

But she had one more favor to ask him. "While you have your assistant on the phone, don't forget, I have to have some fabric samples to take back to New York, or else my cover is blown."

"I've already put Alessandro to work." He kissed the back of her hand. "He tells me the samples from Milan will arrive in a few days."

"Thank you, Giorgio."

"You are very welcome." He reached for the phone. "We can go out for dinner later or else have something brought in."

"Either sounds good."

He nodded and returned to his previous conference call.

Renata stared at him, realizing all his focus was back on business. Well, he was a prince after all. What did she expect? He certainly had more responsibilities than the junior executives she saw running around New York with a phone attached to their ear and several other devices attached to their belts. It would be negligent of him to avoid his country's business, even for a week.

She remembered how easily her own place was running despite her being gone. Of course Flick was doing sales and management only, not design. If Giorgio thought some of her wedding dresses were wild, she could only imagine Flick's ideas. Knowing what her friend thought of holy matrimony, it would probably have an embroidered panel of Edvard Munch's *The Scream* over the bodice and tiny handcuffs stitched in metallic steel gray over the skirt.

Renata stifled a giggle but Giorgio heard her. He winked at her and grinned.

It was like when one of her brothers elbowed her in the solar plexus and knocked the breath out of her. She actually had to suck in air before she swooned off her wedge sandals at His Sexy Highness.

Giorgio had been drawn back into his princely duties and didn't realize what he'd done to her. Since when did a casual smile make her give goo-goo eyes to a man who wasn't paying her a bit of attention?

On the other hand, maybe that was a good thing. She was sure if she looked into a mirror she would be absolutely mortified at her mushy expression.

She mentally slapped herself and escaped with some shred of dignity before she tossed his phone over the balcony and shoved herself into his arms.

She stepped carefully down the narrow stone stairway from their little apartment. The fresh air outside was a welcome relief to her overheated self.

As if summoned by a genie rubbing a lamp, Paolo appeared across from the foot of the steps, trying to look inconspicuous in a village of six hundred people who were probably all related to each other.

"Paolo?" She beckoned to him and he looked around as if she were talking to some other giant security man named Paolo. *Who, me?*

She huffed in frustration and strode over to him. "Honestly, Paolo, you don't need to follow me. Nobody's going to mess with me in a tiny town like this."

He just stared at her. She tried again in Italian. "I will be fine. *No problema.* Go check on *him.*" She waved her hand in the direction of the villa.

"*Signorina, he* is fine. On the phone much time, not go out. But you are here. With me, *no problema* for you."

Paolo was dead serious. Good Lord, a few days of nooky with His Royal Highness and she needed a bodyguard? Besides Giorgio, of course, who was jealously guarding her body whenever he could.

But what possible trouble could she find in a quiet morning of shopping in a small Italian town? "Paparazzi?" she asked.

He nodded seriously.

"You know if anyone bothers me I'll brain them with a bottle of Scciachetrà." She mimed whacking somebody over the head, and his mouth turned up a millimeter or two. Positively a guffaw from anyone else. "Oh, all right." She sighed and rolled her eyes like the worst teenage drama queen. "Let's go." She silently vowed to take him into the pharmacy and spend twenty minutes in the "feminine protection" aisle.

But off they went, Paolo hanging fairly far behind her so she at least didn't have to try to converse with the man in her Brooklyn Italian, which consisted mainly of curses and food items.

She bought herself a nice cappuccino at a café where the barista sketched a heart into the foam with chocolate syrup or something. Paolo, apparently not needing to eat and drink like a normal human being, declined. Then it was off to the stores. Renata found a boutique that had items from all over the Riviera. A length of lace from Portofino for Aunt Barbara, a small model of Christopher Columbus's ship *La Santa Maria* for her father, who had been in the U.S. Navy. A carved wooden Madonna and Child for her mother, who was still asking the Holy Mother to find Renata a husband, and a bottle of *limoncello* lemon liquor for her grandmother, who had given up on Renata and turned to drink. Actually her grandmother had always loved anything with lemon.

She considered buying jars of the famous Ligurian anchovies in olive oil for her brothers, but the idea of carrying four glass jars of oily fish home in her luggage was enough to make her quail. So they each got a miniature wooden version of a ship's figurehead—long-haired and bare-breasted, of course, so all the guys at the police and fire stations could get a yuk out of it.

By then she was famished and collared Paolo. "I'm hungry and these are heavy. You carry the packages, and let's eat."

She picked a quiet trattoria on a side street that had great smells coming from it and dragged him in. *"Mangia, mangia."* Paolo stood awkwardly next to her tiny table, blocking the waiter who was lugging a big tray of soup and antipasti.

"Come, sit." She motioned him into a chair. He hesitated but seemed to acknowledge he was drawing more attention standing like a Roman statue in the middle of the restaurant.

"Grazie, signorina," he muttered.

"You are most welcome. What is good to eat?"

"Here, the fish."

"Ah, of course." No concerns here that the fish had sat in the back of a delivery truck for a dangerous amount of time. "You like *pulpo?*"

His eyes lit up and he nodded. A fellow octopus devotee.

She loved it, too, but hadn't wanted to order it in front of Giorgio since eating the chewy seafood was less than sexy.

"Okay, why don't you order *pulpo* and whatever else you think is good."

The octopus was cut into rounds and deep fried. Renata and Paolo chewed their way through an order. Really, she didn't understand why people hated octopus. When it was fresh, it was almost tender.

"Good octopus, right, Paolo?"

He nodded.

"Does your boss like octopus?"

He finished chewing and gave her a considering look. Probably he'd been pumped for information before about Giorgio, but decided his master's preference for invertebrate seafood was not a state secret and nodded. The few days she'd spent with Giorgio were much more juicy than his eating habits but she wouldn't be one to blab.

The soup was tomato based with seafood and herbs with fresh garlic toast rounds plopped right on top and the main course was a whole fish cooked with white wine, lemon and herbs.

"He like this soup," Paolo offered. "We make this at home."

"It's very good." She noticed how Paolo never mentioned Giorgio or Vinciguerra by name and figured it was part of security. "What else do you eat at home?"

"Our part is more *del nord*—north. We like polenta, sausage, much butter and *crema*. Meat roasts and risotto. Good food."

It was the longest speech she'd ever heard. Food was close to his heart. "You should write a cookbook for recipes from—" She'd almost slipped and mentioned Vinciguerra. "From your home."

He made a self-deprecating sound. "Nobody need a cookbook. Everybody know how to cook."

"Oh, no, we don't." Renata had to be the only Italian-American girl in New York who could goof up a pot of pasta. "Think about it. Everybody thinks Italian food is spaghetti and meatballs. You could do something different."

"Okay, *signorina.*" He was humoring her.

"Look at me, Paolo. Does New York need another dress designer?"

He shrugged in puzzlement.

"I'll tell you—it doesn't. But I didn't care. And now the, um, other signorina has a nice dress and is very happy."

"Yes, is true. She tell me so. And tell me, and tell me."

Renata snorted with laughter. Ol' Paolo had a sense of humor after all. "I'm glad to hear it. A beautiful girl."

"Si, si." They smiled at each other at their mutual fondness for Stefania.

Renata took a sip of coffee but declined dessert, having filled up on the delicious focaccia in addition to the rest of her meal. If she stayed in Italy much longer, she was going to get a shape like her grandmother, who resembled a Magic 8-Ball in her black dresses.

Ah, well, all the walking and romping around with Giorgio would help. He'd shown no signs of slowing his pace, so she was running out of new lingerie to show him. She'd passed a pricey boutique earlier—maybe that was the place to go.

She set down her cup. "One more stop and then we can go back."

Paolo nodded placidly, as if it were his life's dream to follow her around Vernazza like some giant shopping cart with arms. There was a brief tussle when she tried to pay for lunch but apparently having a woman pay for his meal was more humiliating than carrying her packages. Renata gave in, figuring Giorgio would reimburse him.

She found the place she was looking for a couple blocks away. Paolo gave the display of bras and panties in the window a wary look.

"Don't worry. You don't have to go in."

"Grazie, signorina." He parked himself against a wall across the way where he could see the entrance.

Renata walked into the shop and immediately saw a bunch of possibilities. Racy, demure, corsets, nightgowns, garters, lace, satin…she pulled out her phone. "Hey, Flick, I'm standing here in a lingerie store and don't know what to buy."

"Something sexy, of course."

"Well, duh, but what?"

"What did you bring with you?"

"A bunch of fancy bras, all my garter belts and a corset."

"Okay, so you've got the slutty look covered, let me think."

Renata made a sound of protest at the "slutty" bit but in the end had to agree.

"How about the total opposite?"

"They don't sell flannel nighties here, Flick."

"Not that. You'd sweat to death. How about a nice demure pure white nightgown, as in the 'please be gentle with me, it's my first time' look."

"Ah, the virginal wedding night, but isn't that a bit cliché?"

"No more so than running off to Europe with a hot Italian guy. Trust me, 'Virgin Princess' is the way to go."

Renata snorted. "Guys do love that, even if they know better."

"It lets them pretend they're breaking new ground, so to speak."

"Okay." Renata moved to a billowy rack of white garments. She pulled one off the rack. "Honestly, Flick, this first one here looks like I should be fleeing the manor on the moors in gothic-y terror as the brooding lord chases me."

"That's the idea, dummy. If the gothic-y chick has any sense, she'll pretend to twist her ankle on a rock and let Lord Longmember catch her."

"Really, Flick. Lord Longmember?" she muttered into the phone.

"Or Laird Lang-member, if you prefer the Scottish fantasy. What's under his kilt gives new meaning to the phrase *auld lang syne*."

Renata groaned and reached for another gown. "Hey, this looks promising."

"Send me a pic."

Renata hung it back on the rack and took a quick picture and emailed it to Flick. "What do you think?"

"Positively diaphanous."

"Yep." The nightgown was a sheer white silk with blousy three-quarter sleeves and a satin ribbon fastening the neckline. The gown was cut on the full side but that didn't matter since it was practically see-through.

"You *have* to buy it. 'Oh, milord, I do not understand all these strange new feelings in my forbidden places. Are you ill? You have the strangest swelling in your trousers. Ooooohh.'" Flick made a noise as if she were about to swoon.

Renata cracked up. Her aunt Barbara loved books like that, and Renata had "borrowed" them when she was younger just to read the racy parts. Hmm, maybe that was where she got her taste for hot, dark and handsome upper-crust men. On the other hand, Giorgio would be to any woman's taste. Yum. "Okay, I'll get it. Never hurts to change things up a bit."

"Wear your hair down with some hanging in your face so you can peep from behind it like that blonde starlet. What was her name?"

"Veronica Lake," Renata answered promptly. "Cool, Flick." She'd enjoy this—and of course so would Giorgio.

"Thank you," her friend said smugly. "And about my gigolo? What flight does he arrive on?"

"Sorry, I can't in good conscience send a poor innocent like that into your clutches. How about a nice ceramic vase?"

Flick's response would have shocked a real gigolo but only made Renata laugh. "Okay, no vase. I'll find you something else." Renata spotted the saleswoman who had been lurking nearby straightening piles of panties. "I'll let you know how it goes."

"And in excruciating detail," Flick warned her. They said their goodbyes and Renata carried the nightgown to the counter to pay for it. After mentally calculating the euro-to-dollar rate, she winced but put it on her credit card. She probably had enough cash from Giorgio, but that was her present to him.

The saleslady wrapped it in a white box with matching white satin ribbon. Renata supposed that made sense since it looked like a wedding present. She tucked it under her arm and rejoined Paolo outside. "Ready?"

"Of course, *signorina.*"

She sighed. "You can call me Renata, Paolo."

The look of horror on his face made her fight back a smile. It was practically the first real emotion she'd seen from the man since they'd met.

"I cannot do that, *signorina.* Much disrespect for you and disgrace for me."

"Really?" She tipped her head to the side as they started down the narrow cobblestone street. "But I am not exactly in a position of respect here—traveling with the, um, boss." She'd almost forgotten and said "prince" in public.

Paolo shook his head. "He say I will serve you as I serve him. *Molto rispetto* for him—and you."

Renata nodded. Feudalism was alive and well in the Italian culture, even in her own watered-down New York version. What the guy in charge said, went. If you showed disrespect for someone the boss approved of, you showed disrespect for the boss. She got it.

"Do you think the boss will be finished with his business now?" She had something in mind for an afternoon siesta.

"Si, signorina." Paolo turned a corner through narrow houses and led her back up several narrow sets of stairs.

She was pretending not to gasp for breath when she heard an annoying male voice with a thick Italian accent catcalling. "Eh, *bella ragazza!* Give me a kiss, red-hair girl."

Renata looked around, pissed off. She had enough hooting and hollering at her living in New York, and the Italian version was just as bad.

"Come up here, pretty lady, and I show you good time, huh?" That was followed by several loud smooching sounds.

She tipped her head back and was about to give the man an international gesture when she saw Giorgio grinning down at her from the terrace. "What do you say, gorgeous?"

"I say, 'Okay!'" She opened the door and climbed the stairs to the second-floor living room. She gave Giorgio a quick kiss and made a beeline for the bedroom. Renata the Innocent Virginal Maiden was about to make an improbable and unprecedented return.

10

"Is the signorina all right, Paolo?" Renata had disappeared into the bedroom with an armful of packages and hadn't reappeared yet. Maybe she'd gotten a bit of sun or was unpacking her finds.

"She seemed fine, *signor*. Although she did ask me to call her by her first name." Paolo looked as if that request were enough to doubt her mental capacity.

"And you complied with her request?"

"Signor!" Paolo appeared torn, as Giorgio knew he would. His natural formality and knowledge of what was proper conflicted with obeying a request from his prince's current lady friend.

Giorgio let him stew for a second before letting him off the hook. "You of course told her why that was not possible."

"Si, si, I did." Paolo would never slump with relief but relaxed slightly.

"Americans are very informal, as you know. It can be quite appalling how much personal information they share with each other on merely a short acquaintance."

He nodded eagerly. "That is so true, *signor*. The other drivers I met in New York…" He winced. "I am not a *dottore, signor.* Why do they think I want to know about their prostate problems?"

Giorgio winced, as well. "Paolo, you've had a busy day. Why don't you have a glass of wine at the trattoria across the street? The *signorina* and I will be staying in this afternoon."

Paolo nodded and left. Giorgio headed to the bedroom. He wasn't sure what awaited him on the other side of the door, but was eager to find out.

He tapped on the door. "It's me. May I come in?"

"Of course." Her voice was sweet and soft, and he grinned in anticipation as he twisted the doorknob.

"Mamma mia!" The exclamation escaped him just before his jaw dropped.

Renata stood next to the four-poster bed wearing something that looked like it had floated down on a cloud. She raised her hand to delicately stroke a post and the thin white silk outlined the curve of her breasts, the thrust of her nipples. He could see nothing but was seeing everything. And that up-and-down stroking was enough to drive him mad.

"Do you like it, Giorgio?" She tipped her head and gave him a coy look from behind the curtain of her luxurious auburn hair.

"What do you think?" He stripped off his shirt and yanked his belt loose.

She ducked behind the other side of the bed before he could finish undressing. He moved opposite her once he was naked except for his boxer shorts, ready to dive across if need be. "Why don't you come here and let me show you how much I love it?"

She gave him a wide-eyed look. "I need you to show me so many things."

"Ohhhh." He nodded in understanding. She was taking things in a different direction, aiming for a little role-playing with her in the lead role as Innocent Virgin. Although the droit de seigneur, or right of the lord to de-flower local lasses, never existed in Vinciguerra and was largely mythical elsewhere, the blood of his conquesting ancestors surged in his veins, his cock hardening even fur-ther at the bawdy suggestion.

"I am Giorgio Alphonso Franco Martelli di Leone, Hammer of the Lion and Prince of Vinciguerra," he in-formed her, using his formal family name and all his royal hauteur. "Your duty is to please your prince—and obey whatever he orders you to do."

Her eyes flashed at the obedience part but she lowered her head. "Yes, Prince Giorgio."

"Come here." He thought about snapping his fingers but figured he was pressing his luck.

She glided to him. The afternoon sun slipping in through the shutters totally illuminated her body. Her breasts swayed over a narrow waist and round hips.

"I should rip this gown down the front for you daring to wear it in front of me. It is against the law to appear in the Prince's bedroom with clothing on."

She muffled a snicker.

"But since it is so sheer, I will make an exception for you." How far was she willing to go for this mutual fan-tasy? If she balked, he'd stop, but if she didn't... "Put your hands behind your back."

Renata complied but her expression was confused. He grabbed a necktie from the back of the chair and wrapped it loosely around her wrists, then to the bedpost. Her eyes widened, although she didn't protest. In fact, her breathing quickened and her nipples hardened against the silk.

He moved close so her gown brushed his body, the silk resting on his erection. Oh so close to shoving up the night-gown and taking her how his ancestor would, with thoughts only for his own pleasure, the smoothness of her thighs, the hot, wet tightness of her flesh enveloping him as he pounded deep inside her. And to do it again whenever he felt like, to have her ready and willing at any time of the day or night. The good old days…he bit back a groan.

"What are you going to do, Prince Giorgio?" Her words held a challenge and he answered it.

"Whatever I want." He smoothed his hands over her breasts, admiring the plump weight as he stared at the dark round nipples showing through the fabric. "And before long, you will beg your master for his touch, his mouth, his cock." She inhaled sharply at his promise.

He covered a nipple with his mouth and she pushed her head against the bedpost, arching her back. "Oh, Giorgio."

He worked the tight nub with his tongue and teeth, the silk a flimsy barrier to his determination. She gave a little gasp and he smiled in pleasure. Her breast felt different under his mouth, cool and wet at first but then hot as his breath and her skin heated the fabric.

He moved from one breast to the other, leisurely exploring their curves through the intriguing veil. Renata wiggled in his embrace, a bead of sweat trickling down her neck between her breasts. He licked the salty trail until it fell below her neckline.

Giorgio sat back on his haunches. What would his ancestor do? He gave her a long, slow grin and put his hands on her neckline. "I will buy you another."

"Another what?" Her dazed eyes widened and she squealed as he ripped the nightgown right down the middle. "Giorgio! Do you know how much this cost? The dollar-to-euro conversion is terrible this week!"

"I will buy you, ten, twenty of them," he swore as he followed that intriguing droplet of sweat down her belly to where it pooled in her navel. Ah, just right for his tongue.

"And I thought bodice ripping was the stuff of myth and legend," she quipped, breaking off into a long sigh as he licked her belly.

He had no idea what she was talking about since he was dizzy from her scent, intoxicated from the feminine musk rising from her arousal. He gently spread her folds and dabbed his tongue onto her clit.

She stopped a scream and sagged against the bedpost.

"Here." Not wanting her to fall, he lifted her onto the mattress, and raising first one leg over his shoulder and then the other, supporting her weight. Her hands were caught loosely enough to take any pressure off her shoulders.

Once she was comfortable, it was time to go to work pleasuring her. He returned to his previous position and opened her wide to him. She had an attack of uncharacteristic shyness and brought her legs together.

"None of that." He stroked her breasts until her knees fell apart.

"Giorgio," she sighed his name. "This is so…so…" She stopped, unable to find the words for her thoughts.

"Arousing? Sexy? Incredibly hot?"

She swallowed hard. "Yes. This is amazingly erotic. I feel like the lord of the manor is preparing to ravish me."

"Good. Then you have the right idea. You will be ravished." He bit her smooth neck, careful not to mark her white skin. "Totally." He suckled one nipple to a plump red peak, pleased at her moans. "Completely." He nipped the other, tugging until it swelled to match. "And quite thoroughly." He dipped his tongue into her soft, sweet belly button, so glad she had pale, lush feminine curves instead of a stringy boyish build.

She raised her hips in invitation, which he accepted, staring at her again. She was beautiful in her feminine secrets, medium pink like the inside of a conch seashell, her hidden pearl peeping out as it swelled with arousal.

He inhaled her musky scent eagerly. He couldn't stop remembering how she had gone up in flames under his mouth in his limo and had been eager to see if she would respond like that again. Her thighs quivered in anticipation.

"Do you know how pretty you are here?" He traced his finger around one petal, then the other, purposely avoiding her clitoris.

"No, I never thought much about it," she panted. "But you can show me your appreciation in one very special way."

"Oh, I will." He kept up his lazy tracing, spreading her juices freely. She plumped up even more under his touch, darkening to a deep rose. "In many special ways."

He slid a finger inside her passage, smugly noting how she instantly pulsed around him. He leisurely thrust in and withdrew, mimicking what he would do later with his cock.

A second finger joined the first.

He rubbed a slightly raised slick spot and she gave a short scream. "Oh, my God, Giorgio! What is that?"

Thrilled that he was teaching her new ways of pleasure, he kept fucking her with his fingers. She attempted to move him along faster by wiggling her bottom, but that made him stop, increasing her frustration.

"Gently, sweetheart. You are always so impatient. Must be that New York temperament of yours."

She strained at her soft bonds. "You can't just tie me up and tease me like this. I want you to make me come now."

He inspected her carefully. She was frustrated but not frightened by their sex play, and he had noticed her pussy dampen and her nipples tighten with lust every time he mentioned the neckties.

"Dammit, Giorgio."

"Careful, my innocent maid. I may tire of your complaints and decide to quiet you."

"What with? Another one of your fancy silk ties? Why did you bring so many on a vacation?" Her breath was coming faster and harder the deeper they fell into the fantasy.

He laughed. "Why would I use a silk tie? There are much more pleasurable ways to fill your mouth." He deliberately rubbed his cock along her leg.

She stared at him, wide-eyed, a fresh slick of moisture running over his fingers. An answering drop soaked into his boxers. He desperately wanted to open his shorts and show her exactly how he could fill her mouth, her hands, her pussy...having her tied up and screaming with pleasure as he took her until his cock exploded.

Merda! His civilized veneer was paper-thin around this woman. With her hair falling down over her magnificent breasts and her nightgown in shreds, she was arousing his previously dormant pillaging and ravaging urges. The Princes of Vinciguerra had long been a hard-fighting, hard-loving lot but he thought modern life had stamped those characteristics out over the past several decades.

Apparently not. He counted to twenty in Latin and calmed down enough to move back between her thighs.

This time, he didn't stop once he'd rediscovered her G-spot with two fingers and watched with strained satisfaction as she climaxed quickly, pulling at the ties in ecstasy. Red-faced, sweaty and gasping, she was the most beautiful woman he had ever seen.

He knew she had more response left, so he stroked her clit experimentally. Plump and swollen from her powerful orgasm, it quivered under his touch.

And under his tongue.

He inhaled her scent greedily as he buried his face deep.

Her clit rolled easily in his mouth, pulsing as he sucked her gently. She sobbed his name when he rolled his tongue around her passage, dipping inside it as if it were filled with sweet nectar.

"Oh, Giorgio, yes!" Her hips bucked under him, and he scooped his hands under her round ass to hold her still for his mouth. His cock was twitching and jerking like mad; a flick of the wrist and one quick thrust and he could possess her lush, moist pussy with it. She would eagerly submit to him and probably immediately climax, squeezing him in her hot depths as he pulsed within her.

But he would wait. Just a little longer. He gave a long groan of frustration and she pushed against his face, crying out as he rubbed his lips over her. Her legs trembled and she sucked in a deep breath. He sucked hard on her clit and she shrieked her release, thrashing into him as he penetrated her with his tongue, aching to do the same with his cock.

He held on to her until she stopped shaking and sobbing.

"Giorgio," she whispered.

He raised his head and gazed up at her, worried that it had been too much for her.

But then she smiled at him, and a wave of affection passed between the two of them.

"Renata, are you all right?"

"Fantastic." She rolled her shoulders and he quickly undid the ties.

"Are you sure?" he asked anxiously, trying not to get distracted by her satiated nudity.

"Absolutely. You high-handed princes know how to show a maiden a good time." She stood and ran her finger down his chest, swirled it into his belly button and then stopped right above his waistband. "And now it's time for the maiden to show the prince." She snapped his waistband.

He gulped. For the first time in known history, a Vinciguerran prince would be the one getting ravished. Thank God for modern times.

RENATA STIFLED A GIGGLE at the look that passed over Giorgio's face, half relief and half nervousness. "Sit." She pushed him toward the upholstered chaise and he sat like a king on his throne.

His black silk boxers were strained to the limit in the front. A quick flick of her finger and his erection popped free. Wow, that was sexy-looking, his desire too much for even his clothing to contain. His pupils dilated and then contracted as he stared at her in silent anticipation.

She dropped to her knees in front of him. "Let your loyal subject please you, Your Highness." She deliberately put her hands behind her back as if she were still bound.

His mouth opened in shock at her submissive posture. "Renata, no." *No,* her ass. He'd been fighting his desire to dominate, take her, penetrate her, so much he'd been shaking.

She brushed her lips over his cock and then he wasn't protesting anymore. He dropped his head back against the upholstery, his mouth opening in a groan. "Ah, *si, si...*"

She lifted her head. "Your Highness, I want to please you. Show me what to do."

His eyes blazed green and she could tell he was at the edge of his formidable control. Considering what he had done to her while she was tied to a bedpost, she figured that was an even exchange. She deliberately ran her tongue around her mouth and he cracked, tangling his fingers in her hair.

"Take me in your mouth. Now."

She opened her lips and he thrust inside. She meekly accepted him, waiting for him to instruct her further. He moved her head up and down on him, his cock growing hotter and tighter. She fought the instinct to participate more actively but the juicy, fat head slipping along her tongue was starting to turn her on, too.

"Harder," he gritted out. "Suck on me."

His wish was her command. She immediately applied suction and he went wild, digging his strong feet into the carpet and boosting himself deeper. She relaxed her throat and flicked her tongue along the base of his shaft, humming in appreciation.

His skin was hot and taut under her lips and tongue, a salty drop coating his flesh. Renata sucked hard and felt him harden further.

"Ah, Renata, more, more…" He relaxed his hands and she lifted her mouth off him.

"Tell me, Your Hardness, who's in charge now?"

His gaze was blurry with desire. "You are, Renata. You always have been." Before she could blink, he pulled her onto his lap and shoved her nightgown up to her waist. She automatically spread her legs for better balance and he prodded her slick passage with his erection. "Release me from my misery, sweet Renata."

She sighed with satisfaction and sank onto his cock, moving up and down on him. His hands tightened on her ass and a flash of brilliance popped to her sex-soaked mind. "Spank me."

His eyes flew open. "What?"

"You heard me. Just a tap, okay? I don't want to have trouble sitting tomorrow. Don't you think it would be hot?"

"Si." His voice was raspy, as if his mouth were dry. "Very hot."

He lifted his hand slowly and smacked her bottom.

She let go with a shocked puff of air. He looked at

her anxiously until she smiled. "I'm not going to break, Giorgio."

"I would never hurt you, Renata," he promised.

"This is for fun, not hurt."

He did it again and this time, she was ready, moving up and down him as his hand landed on her. She shuddered, this time with naughty arousal.

Giorgio grinned. "You just tightened down on me. What a bad girl you are, Renata, darling. I should take my cock out of you and put you over my lap for a good spanking."

"Sorry, Prince Giorgio," she said in a falsely meek voice, knowing that she'd just spasmed around him again at the image of her spread over his lap, his dick pressing up into her breasts as he reddened her bottom.

"For punishment, play with your nipples. I like to see them pink and plump—just like your pussy." He punctuated that with another light slap.

She cupped her breasts, teasing herself with light and then firm touches until her nipples were hard and red as rubies.

From his answering groan, it was punishment for him, too. His eyes were heavy with lust as he watched her avidly. "Very, very risqué, darling. You like to touch yourself, don't you?"

"Mmm." She was having a hard time catching her breath.

"Of course you do. Next time, I want you to sit in this chair and show me how you like to play with yourself. Maybe I will do the same. After we met and I was waiting for you to arrive, I couldn't stop remembering your naked wet body under mine."

"What did you do?" she whispered.

"Wrapped my hand around my cock and thought of you. Many times. In the shower. In the morning. At night. You stripped my self-control. And now it is not any better." He sounded almost angry. "I smell your perfume, see the curve of your neck and can't think of anything but ripping your clothes off and fucking you."

He stopped talking and put action to words. She thought he'd wrung every bit of pleasure out of her earlier, but she was wrong. He reached down to play with her clit as she lifted herself up and down on him.

Oh, he felt so good, inside and under her. She closed her eyes to revel in the sensations he was building in her but he called her name.

"Open your beautiful blue eyes. I want you to look at me when you come."

She gulped. That seemed even more intimate than some of their previous activities.

He stopped caressing her. "I mean it. No dress-up or games. Just Giorgio and Renata, together."

She bit her lip and nodded.

"Good." He sat forward and wrapped his arm around her waist. "Move on me, lovely Renata."

She did, her breasts brushing his face until he captured one in his mouth, his fingers toying with her clit. The delicious pressure built again. Her back bowed and he let go of her nipple.

"Look at me!"

She forced her eyes open to see his fierce expression. He was barely restraining himself and that made her even hotter. She wiggled on top of him and he pinched her nipple, rolling it under his thumb.

She clamped down on his erection and he let go with a stream of very slangy Italian telling her exactly how she was tormenting his cock and how his balls were about to explode. He also threatened to spank her again and she involuntarily spasmed around him.

He began to laugh. "Eh, so you understood that." He

gave her a little slap on the ass and it was all over for her. She crumbled to pieces. Her climax overtook her.

He dug his fingers into her hair. "Look at me," he gritted.

She did, gasping, sweating, captured by his cock and his hands even more effectively than when she'd been tied to the bedpost.

His nostrils flared at her capitulation. "Oh, yes, that's it." He heaved a sigh and she saw how he surrendered to his own orgasm as easy as stepping off a diving board into a pool.

He clenched his jaw and pounded into her, his groans growing louder and louder as his seed jetted from him. His gaze was locked onto hers like a laser and she instinctively knew this was a part of him he had never shared with another woman before.

She wrapped her arms around him and rocked back and forth in time with his movements until he slowed. Before he could say anything, she pushed forward and caught his mouth with hers. Their lips clung for what seemed like forever and then he broke the kiss, resting his forehead on hers as they caught their breath.

"Oh, Renata *mia,* just when I think this cannot get any better, you prove me wrong."

"I thought you'd like that nightgown."

They both looked at the remnants of that poor abused garment, bunched around her waist and covering his like a see-through loincloth.

"I will have to buy you many more."

"For a modern monarch, you sure do have archaic tastes in the bedroom," she teased him. "Tying up an innocent maiden, forcing her to satisfy your debauched lusts and beating her when she was too frightened…"

He eased out of her. "You call that a beating?" He stood

and scooped her into his arms. "I think milady doth protest too much, as the playwright said. I think she just protests because she liked it *too* much."

Renata flushed and hid her face in his shoulder. He was right. She never would have even tolerated a spanking from any other man, much less enjoyed it so much. He laughed uproariously and set her on the fresh, cool sheets of the bed.

"Giorgio, I'm a mess!"

"A lovely, well-satisfied mess." He tugged the night-gown down her legs and tossed it on the chair. "Your monarch needs *un reposo* and will be very cross if his favorite maiden doesn't join him for some sleep. I plan to stay up for a late dinner and an even later bedtime." He crawled into bed next to her. "You Americans should try an afternoon rest. It does wonders for your disposition." He pulled her back to him so they were spooning and draped an arm over her waist.

"You do wonders for my disposition," she admitted. "You may not believe this, but some people think I can be difficult."

"No!" He spoke the denial with such shocked sincerity that she looked over her shoulder in suspicion. He quickly hid his expression by kissing the nape of her neck.

"Hmmph." She muffled a snicker, which turned into a yawn. "As punishment for your sarcasm, you can take me out to the nicest restaurant you can find."

"Only the best for you, *principessa mia*." He yawned, as well, but Renata's eyes flew open. He'd just called her his princess. From a regular guy, that wouldn't mean a thing, but from him?

She slowly shifted to face him but he was fast asleep already. A slip of the tongue, no doubt. It wasn't as if he were offering her the job. She sighed. That was how things got sticky—the girl started imagining herself in a hip, yet lovely wedding gown while she doodled *I HEART PRNZ GIORGIO 4EVR* or *PRNCS RENATA RULEZ*. Literally.

Well, no more of that. Despite how hot, sexy, sweet, kind and wonderful Giorgio was, Renata would not fall in love with the man. Giorgio might like her adventurous Brooklyn personality for a fun vacation, but not permanently. No, when he finally settled down, he would want a sweet, delicate woman who could bake him lemon cookies, wave at crowds and never think of wearing a diamond in her nose or embroidering tiny skulls on a wedding dress. Renata wasn't princess material. Her heart was still packed away in acid-free tissue and a big fancy box, just like one of her vintage wedding gowns.

LATER THAT EVENING, Renata poked her head out of the bedroom. She could hear men's voices in the living room. Many men. She followed the voices.

She clutched her robe around her when she saw how many guys there actually were. Giorgio glanced up at her from an intense photo conversation and lifted his finger in a "wait a minute" gesture.

She turned to the beefy guy standing next to her. "What's going on?" she whispered.

He turned his head to stare at her with blank brown eyes but didn't answer. Maybe he didn't speak English, or maybe he wasn't paid to speak.

She retreated into the bedroom and dressed hastily in a button-up white blouse and denim capri pants, slipping her feet into plain white sneakers. The sexpot look was inappropriate for a serious situation.

She returned to the living room and sat in the floral armchair. Giorgio continued speaking in rapid Italian on the phone, gesturing emphatically. She understood that he was asking about the safety of his sister and grandmother and started to get alarmed.

For once, though, she kept quiet, realizing that she would only at best be a distraction and at worst a nuisance if she pestered him in the middle of his conversation.

He paused to bark orders at Paolo, who pulled out his own phone and made a call as well.

Renata forced herself to stay calm—until the night exploded with noise. A two-hundred-fifty-pound man was pulling her to the ground and covering her with his bulk.

The clattering noise continued in bursts for several seconds. Was some nutjob shooting at Giorgio? They still assassinated princes and prime ministers. She pushed at her own bodyguard but it was as futile as pushing on the wall. She yelled Giorgio's name but the other men were drowning her out as they called information to each other.

Renata slowed her breaths. Finally the noise stopped and she thought Paolo shouted something. Her bodyguard heaved a sigh of relief and eased off her. *"Petardi,"* he said.

"What?"

"Like American Fourth July. Pop, pop, pop." He imitated a string of fireworks.

"Oh, firecrackers." She started to sit up, but he pulled her back down and shook his shaved head. "Well, if we're going to get horizontal together, I should atleast know your name." It was a feeble attempt, but at least it gave her something to think about besides the adrenaline shakes starting up.

He gave her a puzzled look.

"Never mind."

"Okay!" Paolo shouted. "All clear!"

Renata sat up this time and spotted Giorgio across the room. His bodyguards had dumped over the couch and coffee table, sandwiching him between two of them as well as the furniture. He sat up looking mussed but not particularly upset. This must have happened before—maybe even with real bullets instead of firecrackers.

"You okay, Renata?" he called.

"Fine." She lifted a hand to wave at him, and her shakes made it wave on its own. She quickly dropped it.

He looked concerned but lifted his phone again. *"Pronto? Pronto? Si, petardi."* He laughed about how firecrackers could send them all into a state of siege.

Renata wasn't. She didn't think she could stand yet. She scooted so her back rested against the bottom of the chair and pulled her knees up.

Giorgio talked on the phone for another minute and then passed it to Paolo.

Giorgio came over to her. "Are you okay? Giuseppe there is a pretty big guy so I hope he didn't hurt you when he pulled you down." He extended a hand. "Come here."

She took his hand and only wobbled a bit getting to her feet. He guided her to the couch, which was back on its feet as well.

"Giorgio." Her voice quivered a bit. "Giorgio, what is going on?"

He sighed and gestured at the front windows. "That was firecrackers. Probably the local football team won a match, or someone got married, or just teenagers fooling around."

"You have eight huge guys standing in the living room on the remote chance firecrackers go off and they need to hurl you to the floor?"

"No, of course not. These men are the rest of Paolo's team. They've been staying nearby in case of incident."

"What incident brought them all out here? Is your family all right?"

"Yes, and thank you for asking." He lifted her hand to his

mouth and kissed the back. He kept hold of it, his warmth starting to ease her chills. "But there was a bomb threat at home. At the palazzo."

"A bomb threat? Where your grandmother lives?"

Giorgio nodded. "Of course the anti-terrorism squad was deployed immediately with the bomb-sniffing dogs. They did not find anything. But when one member of the royal family is threatened, it is standard protocol to deploy extra protection to the other members in case of muliple points of attack."

"So Stefania has her own team swarming her in New York."

He gave her a sad smile. "Yes, this doesn't happen often, but this is not the first time. My grandmother is probably more annoyed than frightened. She has seen Vinciguerra through worse."

"Worse than bomb threats?"

"She was a girl there during World War II, and during my grandfather's reign many different factions wanted control of the country. We have a natural deep-water port and the original palazzo is a heavily fortified citadel. Violence was not rare."

"Oh." Renata had imagined his country as sort of an Italianate theme park, untouched by darkness or pain. However, one glance at the serious men around her told her that violence was not part of the past. "Who called in the bomb threat?"

Giorgio snapped his fingers and Paolo immediately came to his side. Renata blinked. She didn't think she'd like Giorgio snapping his fingers at her, but the bodyguard wasn't offended by the princely gesture. "Paolo, who did this?"

Paolo replied at length. Giorgio signed at the end of his explanation and turned to Renata. "He says the Vinciguerran police have arrested a local group with anarchist affiliations. Their landlady overheard part of their phone call and put two and two together. They had been acting strangely—even more strangely than usual—the past couple days."

"Anarchists?"

He smiled, which startled her. "One advantage of dealing with anarchists is that they're pretty disorganized. No one is in charge, after all."

"Giorgio!" His gallows humor was disconcerting.

"Sorry, sorry." He put his arm around her. "I know you aren't used to this. We try our best to stay safe, but we have to live our lives without fear."

"You're not scared?" Renata was terrified, disorganized would-be terrorists or not.

He shrugged. "Not for myself, but for Stefania, my grandmother. And you."

"Me?"

"Of course." He kissed her forehead. "I am responsible for your safety. Anyone who tries to harm you will have to come through me."

"And Paolo and the rest of his guys."

"That goes without saying." His eyes filled with pride as he surveyed his team. "They'd do anything to protect us, and I hope to God they never need to."

Renata shivered. Assassination attempts and squads of bodyguards were something from the nightly newscast, not something she'd ever expected to experience. "What do we do now, Giorgio?" she whispered. She meant it as a rhetorical question, but he took her literally.

"Pour us each a glass of wine. Your nerves don't need any caffeine." His phone rang and he snatched it up. *"Pronto. Si."* He listened and gave her a wry smile. "Stefania is safe. Apparently the security team, uh…startled her and Dieter."

Poor Giorgio. Renata was sure he would have rather pretended Stefania and her fiancé spent their time pining for each other, but such was obviously not the case.

Renata hid a grin, but sobered quickly. Not much to smile about. She found a nice red wine in the rack and popped it open. That puppy wasn't getting the chance to breathe—one glass was going straight down the hatch.

11

"WHERE ARE WE GOING TODAY?" Renata was intrigued. Giorgio had told her to pack an overnight bag with swim gear. "To the beach?" She had worn a white peasant blouse over a snug denim skirt and high-heeled slingback sandals with a cork wedge and red snakeskin embossed leather upper.

"In a way." Giorgio, carrying both of their bags, led her down to the pier a block away from the hotel.

"Ooh, a boat ride." A good-size yacht was docked at the end of the long pier. She was glad she'd popped on a wide-brimmed white straw beach hat and oversize Jackie O sunglasses. Sun rays bounced off the water like crazy. And she could always pretend to be Jackie O reading a very serious book on Onassis's yacht. Except she didn't have any serious books and Giorgio was infinitely more interesting than one anyway.

"A yacht. You once suggested I should try it for relaxation. And I wanted to make it up to you for the commotion last night."

She waved a hand at him. "That wasn't your fault."

"If I were a regular man, it would have never happened."

He handed the luggage to a sailor wearing a bright blue polo shirt and helped her up the gangplank.

She recognized that shade of blue. "I think this is the same boat we came on from Genoa."

"Yes, you're right. We're going on a private overnight cruise."

Her eyes widened. "We have the whole yacht to ourselves?"

"Us, plus the captain and a couple crew members, including a chef."

She climbed a set of stairs to the upper deck. He made an appreciative noise and gave her a quick pinch on the butt as he followed her. High heels plus a tight skirt were a killer combo since she'd thrown a bit of extra wiggle into her step.

They emerged on deck where they got a kick-ass view of the harbor with the ocean behind it. "Well, you just dodged a bullet by not having me cook."

"An Italian girl who doesn't know how to cook?" He shook his head in mock dismay and slipped his arm around her waist as they leaned on the rail. "What would your mamma say?"

"She'd say I'd never get a man without knowing how to keep him happy in the kitchen, but…"

He raised his eyebrows. "What?"

"My grandmother would say it's more important to keep him happy in the bedroom." Unless she was baking lemon cookies.

He threw his head back and roared with laughter. "Not to disparage your mamma, Renata *mia,* but I think your *nonna* is correct in this instance." The yacht began to move away from the dock and the salty breeze picked up.

"I agree. It's socially acceptable to order out for meals, but not the other."

"That depends on who you hang out with," he told her.

She screwed up her face. "Yuck!"

"No, not me," he assured her. "Perhaps it comes from having a little sister, but that kind of girl never appealed to me. They are always somebody's daughter—or sister."

"Good for you." She reached up to kiss him. Of course Giorgio wouldn't need to pay for sex, but he probably knew men who did. From what she'd seen on tabloid TV, some girls flocked around rich guys like skimpily dressed moths to a flame.

She had an unwelcome thought. What was the difference between them and her? She was here on Giorgio's dime and had only paid a fraction of what had to be extensive expenses. On the other hand, she had gone out with him in New York because he was gorgeous and fascinating and had never asked him, never even considered hinting that he should take her to Europe. That was *his* idea. She had never been a gold digger and she wasn't about to start now. Besides, he knew she wanted him for sex, not money, and had said so when he called to ask her on the trip.

Maybe that would salve her conscience. She was here because she couldn't get enough of him the man, not him the prince with a royal treasury bankrolling their activities. She would have gladly spent a week in New York doing the same thing they were doing, minus the sightseeing. Logistics and nosy people had made that location impossible.

Renata sighed and looked over the beautiful blue water, the seabirds wheeling above the waves. It was too fine a day to worry. Giorgio knew she wasn't like that, and so did she.

A steward in a white dinner jacket handed them each a glass flute and disappeared. "Ooh, champagne."

"Prosecco," he corrected her. "They grow Prosecco grapes north of Venice in the foothills of the Alps, not too far from Vinciguerra."

"I'm sure I'll love it."

He surprised her by reaching under her hat and gently taking off her sunglasses. "I want to see your lovely blue eyes."

Renata blinked her lovely blue eyes in the dazzling light. Giorgio lifted his flute and she did the same.

"To us."

"To us?" Was there an "us"? At least for the next week or so.

"And our cruise on the lovely Italian Riviera."

Ah, a little bon voyage toast. "To our cruise." She lifted her glass to clink his and then drank. The sparkling wine was fruity and dry with a hint of peach.

Giorgio certainly was showing her the lifestyles of the rich and famous on their trip. She'd been slightly concerned she wouldn't see anything of Italy but the bedroom, but Giorgio, probably realizing she wouldn't be jet-setting back to Europe anytime soon, was being so considerate in arranging typically tourist opportunities.

The yacht slowly began to move away from the dock with a low humming of the engines. "This is really lovely, Giorgio." Her arms settled around his waist as if they belonged there and she clung to him.

He smiled down at her. "Nicest bon voyage I've ever had."

"Me, too." She'd have to get an extra-long bon voyage kiss before she hopped a plane for New York.

"What's wrong?"

Her expression must have reflected her dismay at leaving him in only a handful of days. "Oh, um, the sunlight bouncing off the waves got me for a second."

"Then you need these back. I'd hate for you to get a headache from the sun. It often bothers visitors who aren't used to it." He slipped her sunglasses back onto her nose, and she was glad for the concealment. He put his own pair on. They stared out over the water, each safe from revealing too much thanks to their shatter-resistant dark lenses.

"Where is the trip taking us?"

"Another surprise, but it will involve lots of sun, fun and food."

"Three out of four of my favorite things."

He pursed his lips into an air kiss. "I'm sure we can make time for your other favorite thing."

"What, swimming?"

He laughed. He slid his hand down her waist so it rested on the curve of her hip. "The captain will be down in a minute to give us a tour of the towns as we pass them, but I think after that I will give you a tour of our stateroom. You will have had a bit too much late-morning sun and retire there for a nap—with me, of course."

"Wow, how decadent. A nap already?" She rolled her hip slightly so he caressed her bottom.

"Everyone knows redheads are susceptible to heat," he told her with a serious expression.

She wiggled her eyebrows. "Only to your heat," she whispered as the captain arrived, maritime-spiffy in his white shirt with black-and-gold epaulets. He had sunburned crow's-feet at the corners of his snapping black eyes.

"Ah, Capitano Galletti," Giorgio greeted him warmly.

"*Signor, signorina,* welcome to my ship, *La Bella Maria,* named after my lovely wife, Maria. *Benvenuto!*" He bobbed his head in a respectful nod. "A pleasure to have you join us as we cruise the Cinque Terre. If there is anything we can do to make your trip the most enjoyable possible, please do not hesitate to ask."

"*Grazie, Capitano.* Signorina Renata's great-grandparents came from Corniglia and she would like to learn more about that village."

"Ah, from Corniglia!" His face crinkled into a mass of

wrinkles, his smile the widest one. "I should have known from your beauty. *Signore,* the most beautiful women in Italy are from Corniglia. But do not tell my wife I said so—she is from Manarola." They laughed. That was the village next to Corniglia. He gestured extravagantly at the panorama behind him. "They are so beautiful because of the sun, the sea, the fresh air and the *fish,*" he said in a significant tone of voice.

"The fish?" Renata asked, wondering how a love of seafood contributed to beauty.

"We always knew fish made you healthy and strong. And now the rest of the world knows—but they take fish in pills." Capitano Galletti shook his head at that foolishness. "Pills, pah."

"Indeed," Giorgio said with grave respect. "We are looking forward to some fresh fish. You have an excellent reputation for your seafood dishes."

"But, of course! The cook will prepare grilled swordfish for you tonight—fresh caught just this morning while we were still in bed."

Renata suppressed a grin. They had indeed been in bed, but probably not asleep. For spending so much time in bed, she was awfully tired. A nap like Giorgio had suggested sounded great.

The captain had other ideas, though. "Come, more Prosecco." He topped off their glasses. "I show you the most beautiful coast in the world."

He was as good as his word. After they left the inlet at Vernazza, he showed them a picturesque view of the hills and cliffs studded with coral, white and yellow houses leading down to the pebbly beach.

"And now, Corniglia!" the captain announced like a proud father. "The first Roman farmer here named it after his mother, Cornelia. What a good son, eh?"

Renata stared at the tiny hilltop town, amazed that her great-grandparents had summoned the nerve to leave it for the wilds of New York City. They must have had the mother of all culture shock when they arrived in America early in the twentieth century. She had friends who lived in apartment buildings with more people than the entire village.

Giorgio leaned in close. "It is only a few kilometers' hike from our flat. We will visit before you go."

She nodded, noting how he'd said "our flat" and then followed that up by reminding her she was leaving. Mixed messages? "I'm not looking forward to leaving."

"Me, neither," he admitted. "This has been a little slice of heaven."

"Heaven indeed! Beautiful wine country," crowed Capitano Galletti. "Jugs at Pompeii had ads for white wine from Corniglia. I have a friend there who makes her own wine—*delizioso!* I can get you a nice, nice discount." He winked at Giorgio, who smiled in return.

Renata wondered what Giorgio might have said if the captain hadn't inserted the ad for his friend's wine. She just had to get up her nerve and ask him again when they were alone.

Renata scanned the coastline and stood up straight. "Look, that guy is jumping off the cliff."

"Crazy, eh? Cliff diving." Something in Giorgio's slightly nostalgic tone made her narrow her eyes.

"So crazy you've never tried it?"

"Well..." He shrugged, a mischievous look in his eyes. "I seem to recall trying it once or twice while vacationing with Jack and Frank in the Spanish Riviera when we were in college. I have to confess my wits and judgment were dulled by major quantities of sangria but we all managed to survive without significant injury. Think Frank sprained an ankle."

"Giorgio! I can't believe you did that." Her jaw dropped. The captain suddenly realized he had to be somewhere else and hastily departed.

"I have to admit cliff-diving was my idea."

"Yours? Were you crazy as well as drunk?"

"Frank was both. He was coming off a bad breakup and wanted to jump off a cliff, minus the ocean below. So I told him if he was going to jump off a cliff, he had to take us with him. Jack calculated the angle and velocity to avoid smashing onto the rocks. We all made it into the water, although Frank moved his foot at the last second and wound up spraining it. Water is very hard when you hit it incorrectly."

"Anything for a friend, huh?" That poor guy Frank had been so down he didn't care, his friend Jack had put some scientific method to the madness and Giorgio had coordinated the whole thing like the leader he was born to be.

Considering how Giorgio was the only male heir to the throne and taking care of Stefania, the risk he'd taken was shocking. "I never knew you had that reckless side."

He raised one black eyebrow. "Didn't you?" His tone was low and seductive.

Oh, yes, she did know about his reckless side. He buried it well under fancy Italian suits and perfect royal manners, but it did exist, simmering away like a pot of pasta water until someone turned it up to boil over. She had been the one to heat him up.

He placed a fingertip beneath her chin and leaned over to kiss her lightly with closed lips, thanks to the presence of the crew, who were probably peeping at them. Renata closed her eyes, the sweet, warm pressure promising sensual delights later.

He moved his finger up her jawline. "We men are all reckless, especially where beautiful women are concerned."

"And why is that?"

"The same reason we dive off perfectly good cliffs. The danger. Do we dare to approach the edge? Once we decide to make a move, it is anticipation followed by pure exhilaration. And what will the finish be? Successful, or—"

"Or a sprained ankle or cracked-open head," she finished dryly.

He grinned and raised his Prosecco again. "Ah, but that only gives us war wounds and battle scars that we can brag about. Almost like breaking a leg on the slopes in Gstaad and then sitting in the lodge while ski beauties bring you brandy."

Renata rolled her eyes. And this was why they were destined to be a vacation fling—just another example of their different worlds. He was a Verdi grand opera singer and she was a Frank Sinatra impersonator. He was a fancy five-star restaurant and she like a mom-and-pop hole-in-the-wall hangout complete with red-checked tablecloth and wax-covered Chianti bottle candlestick.

Lunch was a buffet of antipasti, sausages and salami, Italian cheese and fresh-baked focaccia dotted with garlic. One dish Renata had never seen before was the Cinque Terre version of potato salad with small red potatoes, green beans and pesto sauce, but it was delicious. Wouldn't her mother be surprised when Renata brought back a new recipe?

After a dessert of lemon gelato, Renata stretched out on a deck chair facing the ocean. "Ah, this is the life." She was so full she was considering taking a real nap.

Giorgio sat in the adjoining chair and took her hand. "I'm glad you are enjoying yourself. Although Cinque Terre can be the quietest area of the Italian Riviera, being on the water is even more so."

The crewman finished clearing away lunch with the

captain looking down from the bridge in an avuncular manner. He gave them a friendly wave and they waved back.

"Does he know who you are?" she asked in a low voice.

"Probably." He shrugged his shoulders. "Paolo made the arrangements, and he can be very persuasive in convincing businessmen to maintain their confidentiality standards."

She giggled. With his size and intense demeanor, Paolo could convince anyone to do anything. "Well, the captain seems like a good guy, unlikely to alert the paparazzi. You don't want to wind up on the front of the tabloids, do you?"

"I'm used to it. They've been publishing my pictures since my mother carried me out onto the palazzo balcony after my baptism."

"Since you were a baby?"

He preened. "I was very photogenic. Bald, but photogenic."

"I don't like having my picture taken." She shuddered. "Probably a holdover from my overweight Goth days. I used to hide behind my brothers during family photos. Good thing they're all big guys—"

"Stop. I'm sure you were too hard on yourself. Most girls go through an awkward phase. Stefania wore braces for a couple years and spent hours in the bathroom checking for spots on her skin."

"But to live your life in that fishbowl?"

He stretched out his legs. "But we don't live our lives in the fishbowl. At home, when I was young, my mother would bake cookies and dig in the garden and my father would build model airplane kits with me and go fishing in the nearby river. We were just a normal family, except with fancier clothes and more job titles than most."

"You must have had a happy childhood."

"Happier than the latter part of Stefania's." He caught

Renata's hand. "But what could I do about that?" he asked philosophically.

"You did your best, which was better than most young men would have done." Would her brothers have taken her in under the same circumstances. Of course, she decided. They drove her nuts but they were fiercely loyal.

"I did threaten to punch out a photographer once," Giorgio reminisced with a fond air. "He cordered Stefania in a boutique when I was taking her shopping for a prom dress. We had him thrown out of the store."

Renata made a face. Following a teenage girl dress shopping—a career to be proud of. "If I see one of those camera jerks, I won't threaten to punch him—I'll just go ahead and do it."

He gave her a considering glance. "I believe you. But so far on our ocean trip we haven't done anything worthy of the tabloids."

"What a shame." She smiled at him. "When do we start?"

"How does *now* sound?" He gracefully got to his feet and extended his hand to her. "I would carry you to our stateroom but the stairs are too narrow. You will have to settle for holding hands."

She wiggled her finger at him. "All right, but we'll do better than that once we get in there."

"Of course."

He guided her into the stateroom and she was suitably impressed. Bigger than their bedroom in the villa, it had a king-size mahogany bed with a champagne-colored brocade coverlet and ivory sheets. Little gold sconces were hung over the matching nightstands, and a wide dresser stood off to the side. A big, full-length gilt mirror hung on the wall opposite the foot of the bed. It was classic and lush.

"What would you like to do?" she asked him.

"This." He started to undo the peasant style laces on her top and pulled her bodice open. "*Mamma mia,* what is this?" he asked with delight.

"A bustier." White satin to go under her white top. "You like?"

"I love."

Her heart flipped, even though she knew he was just talking about her lingerie. "Good." She yanked her blouse over her head and unbuttoned her denim skirt. It fell to the floor and she kicked it away.

He actually bit his knuckles and groaned. "Why did we bother eating lunch? If I had known this, you wouldn't have seen anything but this room."

She smiled in sly satisfaction. Her second surprise had been the matching white satin thong. When those paired with the bustier and red high heels, it was no wonder Giorgio was already moaning.

He made a grab for her and she ducked away. "No, no, no." She wiggled her finger at him. "You have to take off your clothes, too."

"Fine." He popped a couple buttons on his shirt, making her laugh.

"And then, I want you to sit at the foot of the bed."

He quickly stripped and sat, beckoning to her. "Come here, baby. Giorgio will make you feel so good."

She shivered, knowing he spoke the truth. He was the most generous lover, making sure she came first every time—sometimes more than once. But she wanted to give him a special thank-you for the surprise cruise and if he had to wait a little bit, then too bad.

"Tell me, Giorgio, were you one of those wild princes when you were younger? Did you and your friends Jack and

Frank blow money watching half-naked girls strut around on stage?"

He laughed. "We were amazingly dull. Which is why I think you are so exciting, Renata."

That gave her just the opening she was looking for. "Let me make it up to you. Sit back and enjoy the show." She found a small radio on the nightstand and tuned it to a hard-beating Italian pop song.

"Come here, Renata. I have something for you." It was more a plea than a command. He spread his knees and showed her what he wanted to give her. He was plenty aroused, his cock large and toasty brown like a sweet-tasting pastry and his sac was full almost to bursting. As she watched, a drop rose on his plump tip, begging her to lick him clean. She almost gave in because she loved the taste and feel of him in her mouth, soft skin over hard flesh, slippery but firm. He loved it, too.

She shook her head and started swaying her hips, trying not to giggle. Two-to-one odds she'd fall on her ass if she tried anything too complicated since dance had never been her strong suit and being on high heels was another mark against her.

Giorgio didn't seem to notice her less-than-professional skills, his gaze hungry as she slowly swiveled her butt. She turned her back to him and wiggled more, pleased at his intake of breath.

"Tell me what you like, Prince Giorgio."

"I want that pretty ass in front of me as I pump into it."

She staggered on her heels, the image hard-driving and graphic. Her thong was immediately sopping wet. "What else do you want?" She turned to face him.

"I want your tits in my mouth so I can suck on them while I fuck you with my fingers."

"These tits?" She slowly lowered the satin cups on the

bustier and folded them down. Her breasts were supported by the corseting but totally naked. Her own breath was coming as hard as his. "Like this?" She sucked on her index finger and slowly rubbed the saliva across the tips. Her nipples hardened and deepened in color to a shiny deep rose.

Giorgio groaned and cupped his cock. "Look at what you are doing to me, Renata." His shaft bulged with veins, the head darkened to a rich plum. "Show me some mercy."

She shook her head. "Show me how you touched yourself when you thought of me. Before I got here and you were hot, hard and horny."

He swallowed hard but he obeyed her for once and stroked himself up and down from base to tip, using his own moisture for lubricant.

Her clit was pounding at a crazy pace so she slipped a finger under her thong.

"Stop." His nostrils flared, his pupils dilating with desire. "Come here."

She obeyed him this time, shaking with desire as she stood in front of him.

"You are quite the little tease, Renata, with your bottom and breasts bared for me but not allowing me to touch you."

She grinned and he lifted an eyebrow. "You need to be disciplined for your disrespect."

"Oh, yeah? Whaddaya have in mind?" she asked in her broadest Brooklyn accent.

"This." He gestured to his lap and for a second she thought he meant the obvious, which wasn't a punishment for either one of them. Instead he actually eased her down so she was lying facedown across his lap. She couldn't believe how turned on she was with her bare breasts falling free on one side of his thighs, her bare ass sunny side up on the other and his long cock smack dab in the middle of her stomach.

Her face burned, and not just from being gravitationally challenged. It was so exciting and so shameful, but way more exciting than shameful because it was Giorgio, after all, and she wouldn't be caught dead doing this with any other man. "Have you ever done this before?"

"No," he rasped. "But I can't help wanting to do all sorts of crazy things to you. You are driving me mad. I only think with my cock when you are with me. When you are not with me I only think of how I can please you."

"Enough talk—more action." She rubbed her satin-covered belly over his cock and he groaned.

"Deal."

Their sexual bargain agreed upon, he set out to consummate it. Her breasts were easy targets as they swayed like ripe fruit for the picking. He brushed her nipples, one and then the other, with the lightest of touches. Then firmer passes, more and more until he was rolling her nipples between his fingers. She let out a moan as he unexpectedly pinched her, bearing the weight of her breasts in his hand.

"I would like to make you come by just playing with your tits." His tone was casual, but the way his cock throbbed against her was anything but casual as he continued to play with her. "But to do that, I want to use my mouth on you. You will lie on top of me and dangle your pretty pink nipples against my lips until I decide which one I want to suck first."

Renata couldn't keep her hips from grinding.

"Oh, none of that." He rubbed his hand over her quivering butt cheeks and then suddenly smacked them. She jerked her head back in surprise but not pain. It was more of a tap than anything. "Stay still and you will get a reward."

"You know I will anyway," she retorted. Her "reward" was currently making its presence known against her belly.

"Minx." He tapped her butt again.

"Ooh, when you call me that, I…I…"

He sighed. "I can see this is not arousing enough to sufficiently distract you from side commentary. Perhaps we should stop…"

"Please don't, Your Highness. I promise to be ever so submissive."

His cough sounded suspiciously like a muffled laugh. "See that you are." He stroked her bottom again to the tops of her thighs and pulled her thong aside.

She arched her back again. "Oh, Giorgio." He had slipped his thumb inside her pussy and was rotating it lazily, stretching her sensitive opening. He bumped her G-spot again and she cried out. It was torture, the constant circular pressure, never in the same place for very long and slow enough to drive her crazy.

His other hand found her breasts and he rubbed his hard palm over both nipples at once. She tried to push them against him harder but he was tormenting her with his light sexy touches.

She started gasping for breath. It was all too much, but not enough. She ground frantically against his hand. "Make me come, Giorgio. I need it now."

"Do you?" he asked lazily. "And what will you do for me in return?" He gave her a quick tap on the ass.

"Anything…anything."

"Tell me. I want to hear you say it."

"I'll take you in my mouth. Suck you until you come. Open my body to you and let you do whatever you want."

"Good." He found her clit with his long index finger and flicked it back and forth. He rolled her nipples between his fingers, pulling them to impossibly long peaks. She started to writhe on his lap, burning hot and cold at the same time.

Her tremors grew harder and closer together as he played her with his hands. She was vulnerable but safe, knowing he had ironclad control over himself—and her. "Hurry, Renata," he crooned. "Hurry to your first climax so I can give you another with my cock."

She groaned and succumbed, arching and crying as she came. Her thong was soaking wet and pressing up into her pussy, her breasts throbbing and full.

She barely had a minute to catch her breath before he was helping her up. "Now it is your turn."

He stood and turned to the side. "Look, Renata." He gestured to the long mirror opposite them.

They were perfect contrasts, her soft body white with red, red nipples and a red shadow under her thong. He was tanned and muscular, his erection strong and dark.

She swallowed hard. "What do you want to do, Giorgio?"

"What you offered me. Your mouth and your body. And we both get to watch."

She'd never done that before but her pussy throbbed at the thought. She eased to kneel in front of him.

"There, Renata. Watch the mirror as I take your mouth. As you wrap your pouty lips around me." He turned his head so he could see her reflection.

She did as he asked, her eyes widening as she saw and felt his pulsing cock enter her mouth. She was stretched into the perfect O around him and felt utterly possessed.

He hissed out a long breath as she automatically applied suction. *"Si, si, mia bella."*

Who was that wanton redhead, dressed in red heels and satin lingerie, on her knees watching herself in a mirror as she hungrily sucked on a man's cock? It was beyond raunchy and she loved it—because it was Giorgio.

His gaze met hers in the mirror. "Touch yourself."

She raised her eyebrows.

"I know how insatiable you are, no? You are close to coming already."

He was right. She slid her hand inside her thong and strummed her clit. Her moans excited him even more, and he cupped her head as he thrust into her willing, wet mouth.

Her breath came in short, choppy bursts and she climaxed again, careful not to scrape him. She thought for sure he'd come, too, but he pulled out of her mouth and helped her kneel on the bed, facing the mirror. He quickly moved behind her, even as she was still coming.

He parted her knees and shoved inside. Her moan turned into a scream of pleasure as his cock stretched her pulsing body. She dropped to her hands and knees and panted, but he pulled her upright.

"Watch us," he commanded. "Watch my dick slip in and out of your body." He covered her bare breasts with his hard, hot hands. "Watch me play with your big, round tits."

She did. She watched helplessly as he drove her to the edge of sexual insanity. He thrust quickly, then slowly, pinched her and then stroked her with a featherlight touch.

"Spread yourself open. I want you to see *everything*."

She whipped her head to the side to meet his hard gaze.

He stopped moving inside her and stopped touching her tits. "Do it, Renata." He snapped the back elastic of her thong and tossed the whole garment aside. "Now you can see."

She slowly spread her folds wide and gasped. Her clit was round and hard as a pearl, her pussy dark rose with arousal. Most of his penis was hidden inside her, his heavy balls resting against her ass. As she stared, he withdrew from her slowly, until his shaft sat between her folds and his head rested right below her clit.

He thrust slowly along that groove, his slick tip brushing

her clit. Renata clamped her legs around him and shuddered.

Giorgio cupped her breasts again, moving leisurely without entering her. The purple head of his cock peeped coyly between her legs with every thrust.

"Who do you belong to, Renata?" he commanded, thumbing her nipples. "Tell me. Who does your body belong to?"

"You, Giorgio," she sobbed. "Only you."

"Mine." He nipped her earlobe. "All mine." Those were the magic words because he slid into her, his tip settling deep inside her.

A few more thrusts and she started to shake. "Yes, yes," he hissed. "Come now, but *watch*. Open your eyes. See the wild woman I make you—the wild woman you are."

She was sweaty and messy—but ripe and fabulous at the same time, her eyes hazy and her mouth red from sucking on him. No wonder Giorgio was so turned on by watching her. Together they were incredibly erotic, his thighs bulging with muscle as he pumped into her.

He held a breast in each hand as if offering himself a present, his hands tanned and strong against her soft white flesh. "Touch yourself."

In a daze, she moved her hand down to her swollen clit and plucked the knot of nerves. Her moans grew in volume and intensity until she exploded. She collapsed but he held her upright, one strong arm across her breasts while he played with her clit. She tossed her head back and forth as he licked and sucked on her neck.

Her world shrank to the three of them—her, Giorgio and the mirror.

She'd never tried watching herself climax before and was mildly chagrined at her goofy expressions, but the one expression she couldn't get enough of was Giorgio's.

Hungry and lustful, sure, but tender and affectionate, as well. And when she'd hit the absolute peak, he wore a look of satisfaction and masculine pride, that yeah, he'd been the guy to do that for her.

And she wanted to be the woman to do that for him. She looked over her shoulder and gave him her best come-hither. "Come on, big boy. Your turn."

He sighed happily and pounded into her, grunting with every thrust. It was hard and wild and full and tight. "Look," she reminded him. "Look at how you take me."

He opened his eyes wider and stared at their bodies locked together in untamed passion. *"Che bella, la cosa più bella del mondo…"*

Good, he thought it was the most beautiful thing in the world. So did she.

He stiffened and started to come, trying valiantly to keep his eyes open to see them. He gave up after a couple earthshaking shocks and buried his face in her shoulder, his breath hot and wet on her skin.

Renata stared at herself in the mirror. Who was she, that she could bring a powerful man to such a shuddering climax just by being herself?

It was a disturbing idea that she had such power over him—and he had such power over her. He lifted his head suddenly and their gazes locked. "Ah, Renata." He looked like he wanted to say more but was at a loss for words.

"Giorgio," she whispered, at an equal loss.

He eased from her and kissed her cheek. "Let's rest. Then you can show me whatever amazing swimsuit you packed."

She smiled back, more at ease again. "You've got a deal."

12

RENATA CAME OUT of the bathroom in her brand-new bathing suit she'd bought last summer from a pinup girl clothing website based in L.A. It was a pure vintage look with bright red cherries dotting the white fabric. The bottoms were high-waisted with enough coverage for her ample tush, and the bikini top was halter-style, a knot between her breasts that hiked up the girls quite nicely. It made her look ripe and lush, and she thought it was the cat's meow.

Giorgio obviously agreed. "Swimming is canceled. We're staying in."

"Oh, no we aren't." She skipped by him, neatly dodging his grab. "If we wait much longer, it will be too dark to swim."

He frowned. "All right. But don't you have a robe or cover-up you can wear?"

She raised an eyebrow in puzzlement. "It's not exactly chilly out there." Then she understood his disgruntlement. "You don't want the sailors whistling at me. Don't worry, the captain runs too tight a ship for that."

"Tight ship or not, they are men. And a man would have to be dead not to notice you—the good captain included."

"Aren't you sweet." She went up on tiptoe to kiss him.

"Relax, and help me put on some sunblock." She handed him a bottle.

"You reject my advances and now want me to rub lotion all over you in the privacy of our lovely bedroom? Cruel woman." But he opened the lid and squirted some into his palm.

"Do it here, or else the sailors can watch you slick me up." She pulled her hair into a quick French twist and clipped it into place.

He grumbled at her flip suggestion but did as she asked him. "You do need this sun lotion with your white skin. How did a redhead like you avoid freckles?"

She laughed. "Have you ever heard of Goths?"

"Somehow I do not think you are not talking about the Germanic tribes that invaded Rome during the Dark Ages?"

"No." She grinned, bending slightly so he could rub some into the small of her back. "I used to be a Goth girl. Sad, gloomy rock music, white makeup and lots of black eyeliner. Oh, and black hair."

He spun her around to face him. Wow, he really had something against the Goths. "You...you dyed your beautiful red hair...black?"

Her grin broke in laughter. "Black as yours, but not as nice and shiny since it was from a bottle."

He still stared at her. "But you are perfect the way you are."

She stifled a snort. She had many good qualities but perfection wasn't one of them. "I wasn't very happy when I was a teenager. I didn't want to take the college prep classes that my father wanted me to take and I didn't want to take the secretarial classes my mother wanted me to take. I just daydreamed and doodled outfits in my notebooks all day long."

Since it was *True Confessions* time, she told him the rest. "My mother was always nagging me to lose weight."

He lifted a questioning eyebrow but prudently didn't comment.

"Although I'm not exactly skinny right now—"

"Again, you are perfect. Round and smooth and…and… voluptuous," he announced, triumphant at remembering the precise English word.

"I had about sixty pounds of extra perfection back then. I looked like a black olive, short and fat."

"I love olives." Giorgio folded his arms over his chest.

"So do I. And I loved pasta, cannoli, lasagna, veal parmesan and all the Italian home-cooking that I ate three times a day." She shook her head and laughed. "Come on, three-cheese lasagna for dinner and they expected me to lose weight? My brothers could eat like that because they were either cops or firefighters or training to be cops or firefighters. I was sitting in school all day and sitting listening to Goth rock on my CD player at night."

"So what did you do?"

"I just got sick of black." He gave her a puzzled look. "Seriously, I wore all black every single day. Even Christmas. Some of my black clothes got worn-out and my mother refused to buy me any more. She told me to wear my grandmother's dresses if I was going to dress like an old Italian widow."

He groaned.

"Yeah, I know. Tact has never been her thing, but she had a point. So I took some money and went to the thrift store. And on the mannequin, there was this absolutely gorgeous dress. It was this stunning grayish-blue silk with a tiny waist and fitted bodice and full skirt—the kind of dress you'd wear if your boyfriend got front row seats to

a Sinatra concert. Nineteen-fifties," she added in case he
didn't realize what era she was describing.

"And you wanted that dress."

"Desperately. I fell in love with the dress and fell in
love with vintage fashion. But I quickly learned a couple
things—if I wanted to fit into the originals, I would need to
lose some weight. And if I wanted to make copies, I would
need to learn how to sew. My aunt Barbara was thrilled to
teach me, and I lost enough weight to where I felt better
physically, stopped wearing so much makeup and let my
hair grow out. It was two-toned for a while, avant-garde
for Brooklyn back then, but it's now actually stylish among
some kids."

He nodded. "Stefania had blue streaks in her hair as a
teenager."

"It's practically a requirement when you attend art
school."

"Well, my grandmother didn't care for it. I barely kept
her from getting a tattoo or body piercings."

Renata touched the small diamond in her nose. "She
probably wouldn't like this. My mother hates it but my
grandmother thinks it's great—mostly because it annoys
my mother."

"Your grandmother sounds like fun."

"She's a real pistol—she's reached that age where Italian women just let it rip. Whatever they think comes out
of their mouth. She horrifies my mother and Aunt Barbara
because they never know what she'll say next."

"If only you were an older woman, Renata. That way
you could say what you really mean instead of holding back
your true thoughts." He couldn't even finish his sentence
without cracking into a wide grin.

She swiped at him, but he easily ducked away.

"If only you could speak your mind—I never know what you are thinking." He was guffawing by then.

She grabbed him in a bear hug, her lotioned arms sliding around his waist. "You are a terrible tease."

"Who, me?" He put on an innocent look. "Do I ever arouse your sexy body and then leave you unsatisfied?"

"Not that kind of a tease." She huffed in mock indignation.

He gave her a quick peck on the lips. "If you are not satisfied, Renata, you are sure fooling me."

"Giorgio!" she squawked and pushed him away. "You're making me blush." The heat was creeping up into her cheeks.

"All right, all right. Let me show you the surprise the captain and I have planned for this afternoon."

"You can't possibly have any more surprises for me. I think I'm all surprised out." The past day had been the culmination of an astonishing trip.

"One more, if you promise you won't faint from shock. On the other hand, I could loosen your garments to make sure you're breathing properly…" He leered cheerfully at her.

She rolled her eyes. Considering she was wearing a two-piece swimsuit, the outcome would be less than altruistic. "Is the surprise up on deck?"

"In a way." He grabbed their robes and a couple towels, so it looked like they were going for a swim. She hoped the water wasn't too cold.

They climbed up to the deck and the boat slowed as it passed a rocky outcrop. "Here we are—are you ready to swim?"

"Oh, okay." She was a pretty good swimmer—all the padding in her boobs and ass made her a champion floater.

Giorgio went into the water first and then helped her

down the boat ladder. She flinched slightly at the water temperature, but it was pretty good considering there were probably icebergs floating somewhere outside New York Harbor this time of year.

Giorgio noticed her wince. "How's the water?" He seemed to notice everything about her, even the small things.

"Brisk, I'll get used to it." She moved her arms and legs experimentally.

"Let's swim over to that rock. The captain tells me you can sometimes see interesting fish there."

"Sure." It had been a long time since she'd swum in salt water and she really enjoyed the increased buoyancy. "This is nice, Giorgio." She fell into an easy crawl. He did a lazy backstroke, his long arms and legs holding back so he could stay with her.

"Glad you like it."

"I've never gone swimming off the side of a boat in deeper water like this." It was kind of spooky to imagine a hundred feet of open water below her. Anything could be swimming down there, looking up. *Oh, look, what kind of new snack is that, flailing around in the water? Yum, wonder how that tastes?*

"Giorgio!" She squealed and slapped at the water's surface, splashing him with droplets. "Stop that!"

"Stop what?" he asked.

"Tickling my feet with yours."

"Renata, *cara,* I am a couple meters away from you. How can I reach your feet?"

She yelped at the sensation of something smooth brushing her ankle. "There it is again." She launched herself at Giorgio at the glimpse of a dorsal fin below them. "Oh, my God! Are there sharks here?"

He caught her easily and glanced over at the yacht. The

deckhands were pointing to them out in the water but were smiling instead of screaming in horror.

Renata took a closer look at what was going for a swim with them. "Dolphins," she breathed. A herd, or pod, or squad of dolphins had come upon them and circled around them, their slick bodies gleaming silver under the clear water.

She'd seen her share of dolphins at the zoo and aquarium, but they were a performing poodle version of this wild animal. Moving at incredible speeds crisscrossing each other, they never faltered.

Renata relaxed her grip on Giorgio's arm, doubly glad they weren't sharks because she had probably dug her fingers in hard enough to draw blood. "Have you ever seen them in the wild?"

He shook his head. "Only in the distance from a boat—never to swim with them."

"What do we do?"

"Since we don't resemble a school of anchovies, I think we are safe."

"Safe," Renata echoed. She always felt safe with Giorgio—everything but her heart. "I don't want to be safe."

"No?" He grinned at her. "How did I guess that about you? Come on." He grabbed her hand and took a deep breath. She only had a split second to do the same before he tugged her under the blue water.

Instantly they were in a different realm that muffled their vision and hearing but heightened touch. Despite his assurances, Renata clutched Giorgio as several hundred pounds of marine carnivore slid by, her gasp coming out in a soundless stream of bubbles. He patted her arm and pointed. A mother dolphin and her baby nodded their sleek, round heads at her, their wide mouths silently laughing at the gangly mammals who'd stumbled into their home turf.

The mother nudged Baby toward them, but Renata was running out of air. She and Giorgio surfaced and so did Baby, spraying them with a fine plume from his tiny blowhole. Mamma Dolphin popped up a second later, clicking and squeaking at them.

"Is it okay to touch them?" She'd seen wildlife documentaries where it could cost a limb to mess with a baby and his mother.

"Let me see." Giorgio held his arms open wide and crooned to them in sweet Italian, almost as if he were talking to a human baby. Renata's heart melted as the baby swam to him, chittering at ultrasonic pitches.

"Okay, so now you're the Dolphin Whisperer?"

He laced his fingers through hers and pulled her close. "Italian dolphins like to hear their native tongue. Here, you try."

Holding her wrist with his as if she were a small child petting a dog, he glided their hands along the dolphin's skin. It was slick and rubbery but warm and vital. She let out some chirps and her whole upper body vibrated like the lid of a grand piano during a powerful chord.

Mamma dolphin bumped Giorgio, his testosterone obviously undiluted by the seawater. He grabbed her dorsal fin and she sped away with him, Giorgio's delighted laughter echoing back to her.

The sailors hooted, as well, talking excitedly among themselves. "Giorgio!" she yelled, panicking before she remembered that baby was still with her.

Giorgio looked like a Greek god, frolicking with the dolphin. He was perfectly at ease with the female dolphin, splashing and smiling as she towed him around the cove. He was young and carefree, much as he probably looked before the weight of substitute fatherhood and ruling a whole country fell onto his shoulders.

"Renata!" he yelled gleefully. "Have you ever seen anything like this?"

She shook her head. No, she sure hadn't. Of all the wonderful things she had seen since coming to Italy, he was the most wonderful. In a fancy suit, swimming, or naked, she loved it all. Her heart gave a funny thump that had nothing to do with the baby dolphin butting her in the chest for attention.

Her smile faded into more of a grimace. She was in big trouble. She'd known he was someone special since laying her lustful little eyes on him, but his fine qualities went deeper than his smooth, tan skin.

He blew her a kiss and her heart thumped even faster before sinking. Three more days and she would be winging her way back to New York as—what was that musical theater song? Oh, yes, as the proverbial sadder but wiser girl. Well, she needed to wise up and fast. Starting to fall for one of the world's most reputed eligible bachelors was definitely one of her stupider ideas.

He came whizzing back to her, towed by the dolphin. He glided to a halt, still laughing with joy as the dolphin bumped him in salute before gathering her baby to follow the rest of the pod.

"Ah, Renata! That was so amazing. It was like flying. I've never felt anything like that." He pulled her into his arms for a thorough kiss that earned more catcalls from the crew. He laughed and waved to them before turning back to her. "Okay, I have felt that way with you. Free and happy, without any worries. But not with anyone else."

Oh man, was she sunk. She pasted a smile on her face.

He didn't notice her strained expression as he wiped the water off his face. "I think the baby liked you, too. Did you have a good time with him?"

"He was very sweet, but I thought for a second his mom might drag you out to sea without me."

He wrapped his arm around her waist, his eyelashes clumped together to frame his sparkling green eyes. "Renata *mia,* I would never leave you. I would swim all the way back from Sicily if I had to."

"You're such a charmer," she scoffed. "My mother warned me about men like you."

"I'm not this charmer you think I am. I spend too much time at my desk worrying about work. The rest of the time I am cutting ribbons for grand openings of senior citizens centers and dog pounds." He laughed. "My friend Frank says I should get dog fur and slobber all over my good suit so I can appeal to women."

He needed more sex appeal like the sun needed a flashlight. "Your buddy Frank doesn't know much about women, then."

"I leave that up to him. He can keep his puppy paw prints and I will stick with you." He kissed the tip of her nose. "And you are turning a bit pink right here. Shall we head back to the yacht? I don't want you to get too tired out here in the water."

"I'd hate for you to have to give me mouth-to-mouth resuscitation." She kissed him back.

"That's for later, not in front of the help." His tone was aristocratically arch, the effect spoiled by his quick grin.

She swam toward the boat, her arms and legs heavy from the unaccustomed exercise. Giorgio kept to her pace, making sure she got back safely.

He climbed the ladder first and helped her up, wrapping her in a big towel warmed by the sun.

"All right." She padded along the hall with him. He opened the door to their stateroom and bowed her inside like a fancy restaurant's maître d'.

She gave in to an impulse and caught him around the waist. He held her in his arms and rested his chin on her head. They were a perfect fit together. It was just a hug, but it was at the same time much more than a hug as his heart beat under her ear, his chest hair tickling her cheek.

They stood there contentedly for what seemed like minutes. Renata wished it would never end, but she shivered involuntarily.

He pulled away, his face serious. "Come, Renata *mia*," he murmured in her ear. "Let me wash the salt from your beautiful hair. Then we will rest."

She followed him quietly into the bathroom, where he helped her into a hot shower. He shampooed her hair, his strong fingers rubbing the salt out of her hair. She tried to think of some snappy comment about high-class shampoo boys, but her smart mouth failed her.

It was sensual without being blatantly sexy, and Renata was afraid she would break the quiet companionship that came from Giorgio just taking care of her. Not so he could grope her, because he wasn't. But just because he had noticed she was getting tired and sunburned swimming in the ocean. Because he had noticed she was cold and shivering and needed to wash her hair.

He quickly washed his own hair and got out first, wrapping himself in one of the white terry cloth robes. He grabbed a thick towel and held her hand as she stepped out, as if she were alighting from a carriage.

Renata stood passively as he squeezed the water out of her hair, buffing her body dry until she was glowing. He finished and tucked her into a matching robe. "One last drop." He rubbed his thumb across her cheek.

"No one's ever done that for me." Made her feel so safe and secure, as if she were fragile and precious.

"Taking care of you is my pleasure. Always."

She yawned suddenly, overcome with fatigue from their swim and a bit heavy in the head from a day of the strong Mediterranean sun bouncing off the waves. "Oh, sorry."

"Come to bed. It's time to rest anyway." He straightened the rumpled sheets and tucked her in, kissing her forehead.

"What about you?" He didn't make a move toward the other side of the bed.

He shook his head. "I'm not tired. I need to check with Alessandro if anything needs my attention. Later, you will get my whole attention."

"Good." She took his hand and squeezed it. "Go take care of *your* business now so you can take care of *mine* later."

He threw his head back and laughed, his solemn mood disappearing. "Ah, Renata. I cannot believe how much you make me laugh."

"It's good for you."

"You are good for me." He kissed her fingers. "Look at you, yawning again. Don't worry, I'll wake you up so you don't miss dinner. I will always take good care of you." He slipped his hand free and closed the door quietly behind him.

Renata tried to think about what his unusual mood earlier in the shower meant, but her mind kept wandering to what he meant when he said he would always take good care of her. That *always* was only for a few days more, wasn't it?

13

RENATA HOPPED OUT of bed after another late night and pulled her robe around her naked body. It had been a couple days since they returned from their cruise and she was scheduled to leave the day after tomorrow.

She didn't want to think about it. She shoved her hands through her hair and padded out of the bedroom to look for Giorgio. It was almost an automatic thing, needing to find him, wanting to know where he was. Not exactly the cool, detached Brooklyn girl she'd always prided herself in being.

Mooning over a guy—Flick would laugh to see Renata right now.

She shook her head. "Giorgio?" she called.

The apartment was silent. She poked her head into the living room and small kitchen, but she was alone.

Suddenly the walls pressed in on her. Since coming to Italy, she'd developed a real fondness for being outdoors, even if it was only to sit at the trattoria and eat focaccia while she and Giorgio watched the sunset.

She opened the door to the terrace and flopped down on the canvas-covered chaise lounge. The terrace was private on three sides due to the curve of the hill and had a wooden arbor over the top covered in lush flowering vines. Not much of a difference from lying in bed, but the air was fresh with all sorts of different scents—the salty, fishy ocean, the explosion of red, pink and yellow flowers from baskets and window boxes, and...coffee?

"Giorgio!" She jumped off the chaise and ran to him.

He waved a white bag and a cup holder with two white carryout cups. She ignored the food for the time being and tossed her arms around his neck.

"Hey, hey." He laughed, spreading his own arms to avoid spilling on her. She gave him a big smooch and his mouth quickly changed focus from laughter to sex. No, not sex, more like...affection?

She broke the kiss as quickly as she'd initiated it. "Good morning!" she said cheerfully.

He staggered back slightly as her weight came off him. "And *buon giorno* to you, too. I have to admit, I didn't think I'd get quite this welcome just by bringing our morning meal. Come sit. Eat." He made sure she was comfortable again on the chaise lounge before passing her a caffe latte and pastry. Fresh as always.

"You know, I'll miss this when I go back."

"They are good." He licked a smear of sugar off his finely shaped lips, which distracted her from her thoughts for a second. "But I am done." He set his half-eaten pastry to the side and ate a slice of cantaloupe instead.

"I'll take that if you don't want it." He handed her the pastry and it was just as good as hers had been. "I mean, I won't just miss the food." She gestured to their terraced surroundings as they relaxed on side-by-side lounge chairs. "The whole atmosphere—*la dolce vita,*" she announced. "The sweet life."

"And if I remember correctly, New York does not have *la dolce vita.*"

"New York is more of a *vida loca* place. It's crazy. I get up, grab a granola bar and a cup of instant microwave coffee."

He winced. "Not even a caffe latte from one of those chains?"

"Stop running down coffee chains. I buy one of their overpriced drinks when I can afford it. I drink it on the way to work then switch to water there so I don't spill on the fabric. For lunch I eat a cup of ramen noodles or peanut butter crackers. For dinner I microwave a frozen entrée and try to figure out the bookkeeping and financial software. I work at the shop every day except Sunday when I work at home drawing up new designs or sewing sample dresses for display. Aside from a couple days off at Christmas and Thanksgiving, this is my first vacation in three or four years." She wound down, embarrassed at both her outburst and at how grim her life sounded. More like *la vita suckola*.

"I am sorry you are always so busy. I am not the man to ask about how to slow down and lighten the load. You and I both need to stop and smell the coffee, eh?"

She smiled and made a production of lifting her coffee to under her nose. "Ah, *delizioso*."

He reached over and took her hand which had been holding the pastry. "Ah, *dolce*." He raised her fingers to his lips and sucked the glaze off them. She wiggled her eyebrows at him as he nibbled at her.

Dropping her hand from his mouth, he laced his fingers through hers. "I know I speak for Stefania when I say she would not begrudge you any extra advertising or publicity in regards to having her as a client. I believe she wants to keep everything a secret until she and Dieter make an official announcement. They haven't set a wedding date yet, although she'll likely choose June next year. The gardens at the cathedral are in full bloom then, and she loves the roses there. After that, you'd be welcome to promote your business as an official vendor to the Royal House of Vinciguerra. It may not mean as much to your American clients as it would to some Europeans, but perhaps it would help increase your sales."

"I think Americans are more impressed with royals than the countries that actually have them."

He snorted.

"Oh, I didn't mean it like that."

"No, it's true. In Vinciguerra my so-called subjects treat me as a nephew who needs to be watched closely and talked to sternly whenever necessary." He rolled his eyes. "Don't ever tell anybody this, but my nickname in Vinciguerra was Giò-Giò."

"Jo-Jo?" This tall, elegant prince was called "Jo-Jo"? She fought back a snicker.

"Yes. With a *g*." He spelled it out for her. "Apparently I had trouble saying *r*'s when I was quite small and the local papers picked up on it. It lasted much too long and my father finally made an announcement on my thirteenth birthday that the Crown Prince would be going by his given name in order to preserve the dignity of Vinciguerra. Nobody wants a grown man named Giò-Giò running a country."

"A circus, maybe."

He grinned. "Look at the politics of any small country and tell me it's not a circus. I am the ringmaster."

"Do you enjoy it? I mean, it's not like anybody ever asked you what you wanted to be when you grew up."

"No, that is true. Fortunately, running Vinciguerra is what I'm born to do. Although some people tell me I'm bossy."

"You don't say."

"And certain redheaded ladies enjoy my bossy side."

"Do tell."

She got an attack of the giggles and flopped back on the lounge chair. Quick as a wildcat, he pounced on top of her, nibbling her neck and pulling open the lapels of her robe. "I thought so. Nothing on underneath?"

"No."

"Good. How about *una sveltina?*"

"A what?"

"*La sveltina.* You never heard of that fine Italian custom before? Along with afternoon naps and evening walks, *la sveltina* is practically a national institution. As you Americans call it, a quickie."

"Geez, Giorgio. Well, come on—you know where the bedroom is." She pulled her robe together so they could walk back inside.

"I want to take you right now." He undid his shorts, releasing his erection from the fabric. He held his penis in his hand. "To continue your Italian vocabulary lesson, this is my *cazzo*. My *cazzo* likes you very much and is often a *cazzone* when you are near—a nice, big *cazzo*."

She giggled but squeaked, "Here?" and glanced around. "We're outdoors."

"No one can see us. We're back away from the railing and at one of the highest points in the village. And we have a roof over us." He rubbed his cock on her bare thigh. "I've wanted to do this outdoors ever since we kissed in Central Park."

"Oh, me, too." She quickly opened her legs to cradle him.

"This is your *fica*." He ran a finger over her already-wet folds. "I can tell your *fica* likes me because it is always *succulenta* around me—nice and juicy. And this is your *grilletto*." He rolled her clit between his finger and thumb. "That means 'little trigger' in Italian. I can make your little trigger fire easily, don't you think, Renata?"

"*Si,* Giorgio." Her head lolled back on the chaise as he thumbed her clit and slid his fingers into her pussy—or *fica,* if today was Authentic Italian Sex Day. Seemed like every day should be that day.

He slid down her body and opened her robe with his strong, white teeth. They did have good royal dentists.

"Ah, *molto bene.*" He gazed raptly at her breasts, but then he was a breast man as well as an ass man. She was one lucky girl, having plenty of both.

"What do you call them, *signore?*" she asked coyly.

"Bellissimas." He nuzzled between one and then the other, his hand still working her *fica. "Ti voglio succhiar le tette.* I want to suck your tits." He captured a nipple between his lips, tugging gently.

She clutched his head to her breast, running her fingers through the silky black hair. It curled slightly over his ears and felt like heaven against her skin and especially between her thighs. His eyes were closed as he sampled her, licking and sucking one nipple then the other leisurely until she closed her eyes, too.

He sighed against her skin and moved back up. Adding protection, he slid into her without any more foreplay, but she was ready and more than willing.

"Ah, Renata. You feel so good around me." He started moving inside her, resting his elbows on either side of her head.

She hooked her ankles around his calves. "Just…because no one can see any body parts…doesn't mean they can't… tell what we're doing."

"I know. Doesn't that make you hotter?" He laughed as her body agreed, clamping down on him. "It does, you little exhibitionist."

She couldn't help blushing.

He laughed again. "Even your pretty tits are pink now. Oh, poor Renata. So shy—but your *fica* is in charge now."

She couldn't disagree. Her body was totally the boss of her, but who cared?

He dug his legs into the chaise for better leverage and thrust in and out, sweat running down his temple. His body was taking over for him, too.

She lifted her knees to allow him even deeper access. He grunted with pleasure and fitted himself to the hilt, filling her completely.

For a second, he stopped and gazed up into her eyes. "Renata, this is perfect. I never want to leave you."

She wrapped her arms around his broad, strong shoulders. "Then don't."

He groaned and buried his face between her neck and shoulder. "No, no, I won't."

Renata clung tighter. If only that were true. But enough time later to wonder why she wished for that so much. Falling into his embrace, she kissed his cheek, his earlobe, wherever she could reach as he made her his, really his.

The sun filtered through the green vines, turning their veranda into a secret bower that sheltered the two of them, hiding them from everyone but each other. She was utterly safe in the circle of his arms—but then she wasn't. She had the sensation of standing on the edge of a precipice, safe for the time being, but on the brink of danger.

He lifted his head and stared at her. "You feel it, too, don't you?"

"What?" He couldn't read her thoughts—could he?

"It's never been like this—not with anyone."

"No." She shook her head, her voice failing her after that one syllable. She didn't know if she was agreeing with him or trying to deny it. Taking a deep breath, she closed her eyes and just concentrated on the physical sensations, blocking out the messy emotional ones.

Her fingers pressed into his butt as a signal and he went along with her silent request, starting to move inside her again.

"Oh, Renata, Renata." It came out a long groan. He pounded into her and she wrapped her legs around his waist. Her sensitive nipples brushed over his silk shirt, and she wished he was totally naked. Wished she was naked, too, right out in the open, the sun beating down on them. Where anyone could see them, could see how perfect their bodies fit together, how big and hard and thick he was— and he was all hers.

The exhibitionistic image made her moan.

"What are you thinking?"

She told him what she'd been fantasizing.

He jerked inside her. "You would?"

"Yeah." She blushed again.

He withdrew from her and stripped off his shirt and then his shorts. Totally naked, where anyone with a long-range camera could see him. And they would need a panoramic lens to capture his cock, wet and glistening from where it had just been welcomed inside her burning, throbbing body.

"Giorgio!" She reached for his hand to pull him down.

"Ah, let them see." He tugged her to a standing position and shoved the robe off her arms so she was totally naked herself.

He sat on the chaise where she had been and pulled her on top of him, sliding easily up into her. "Now they can see. They can see your naked body taking your pleasure on top of me—using me as your sex toy, a tool to make you come and nothing more."

She shuddered, lust rushing through her trembling body.

"The world is watching, Renata," he taunted. "The

women want to be you and the men would kill to take my place."

She fingered her clit, brushing his shaft as he ground into her. Faster and faster, she raised and lowered herself. Shivering and crumbling, her breath came in pants. Unlike Giorgio, who wore none.

"Oh, Renata, what a *fichetta* you are." He shook his head in mock sorrow. She knew that one—he was calling her a hot piece of ass. "What if they saw me spanking you?"

She lifted her ass slightly in invitation and his nostrils flared with arousal. He gave her a quick rap. "You asked for it."

She had, and he gave it to her, pounding into her. His hands fell from her breasts and he gripped her butt, playing and squeezing her cheeks as she touched herself. He spanked her lightly. Pressure built up deep inside her, radiating from her nipples down to where his shaft filled her and around to her stinging buttocks.

His face was strained and dark. "Come now, Renata. Show them how a real woman fucks a prince."

His provocative taunt pushed her over the edge and she came hard. Her orgasm triggered his and he gave a loud shout before exploding into her.

Locked together, they clutched each other as Renata writhed on his pulsating cock. He suddenly let go of her butt and stroked her clit. "Go again. I *command* you."

"No, no," she whimpered. He ignored her and circled the throbbing knot, pulling and teasing at it until she sobbed. Leaning forward, he cupped her breast and flicked its peak with his tongue, sucking and nipping at her until she couldn't stand it anymore and threw her head back in a climax more powerful than the first.

Wild, almost animalistic noises came from her throat, startling her with their ferocity. But this was who she was with him—anything he wanted to do to her, she would let him. Her naked body on top of him outdoors was proof of that. If anybody was watching them...she shuddered again a third time, her pussy jerking and quivering around him.

He threw his head back and laughed in sheer masculine triumph. "Ah, if only I could come three times in ten minutes!"

"Shh," she managed before collapsing on his chest.

"I mean it. The only sights of Italy you would have seen would have been your view out the window as I fucked you all day and night."

"You mean you haven't been?" She lifted an eyebrow.

"I cannot help it." He shrugged. "My appetite for you is insatiable, my thirst unquenchable." He kissed the top of her head and eased out of her.

The ocean breeze cooled her overheated nether regions and was quite chilly, in fact. She reached for her robe but Giorgio insisted on walking around the terrace buck naked as he gathered his clothing.

"Geez, who's the exhibitionist now? Won't you be embarrassed if any naked pictures of you get out?"

He straightened from where he picked up his shorts. "I am not particularly vain, Renata, but I have nothing to be embarrassed about concerning my body."

She had to agree, drinking in the sight of him.

He waggled a finger at her. "Ah, ah, ah. You keep looking at me like that and we're back to noisy, naked public acts of indecency."

She fought to restrain herself. "What about your subjects? Wouldn't they be embarrassed?"

Now he was really laughing. "We are an earthy bunch, like the Italians. If there were photos, I would get a round of raunchy jokes emailed to the palazzo, but they would take pride in their ruler's masculinity, so to speak." He stalked toward her, his cock actually hardening again. "The di Leone princes have always had reputations for being, ah, well equipped and well versed in using it."

OKAY, SO THE REST OF THE morning had been taken up by discovering the capacity of the hot water heater—not so much hot water, but plenty of heat.

She had managed to dress in something besides a robe, choosing a frilly teal-green blouse over a white tank top and khaki capris. She was wolfing down a ham-and-cheese toasted panini sandwich that Giorgio had bought from the breakfast pastry café. He was eating an *insalata caprese* made of fresh basil leaves, tomatoes and slices of fresh mozzarella. He'd tossed it with only a little olive oil vinaigrette and had given her several slices of the cheese. The man certainly took his healthy eating seriously. She, on the other hand, was on vacation and would just deal with extra poundage by returning to her ramen and cracker diet.

She set down her water bottle and brushed the crumbs off her blouse and pants. "Did you want to go out this afternoon? We could take a guided tour of the castle or sit on the waterfront drinking *vino*."

"I had something else in mind. Do you have any sensible shoes?"

"You want me to wear sensible shoes? Out where everyone can see me?" She'd been more embarrassed at their bout of semipublic, raunchy sex. She drew her bare feet up on the couch and admired her dark red pedicure. Taking care of her feet was one thing she didn't skimp on. Healthy food, yes, cute feet, no. Maybe she needed better priorities?

He shook his head. "No more of those sexy high heels. You need to wear good walking shoes today."

"I can walk fine in high heels, even on these cobblestone streets." Even if the wine hit her a little hard, she'd just clutch Giorgio's nicely muscled arm.

He shook his head. "Today, we are hiking."

"Hiking?" She raised her eyebrows. Walking, sure. She walked most everywhere since she didn't own a car. Did he mean in those really high hills behind the town? Even the vineyard workers took a special elevator/train up to the grapes. "I'm more of a pavement girl."

He burst out laughing. "What is the American saying? You can take the woman out of New York City, but you can't take the New York City out of the woman. The people I talked with assured me that some of it is pavement. You did not bring walking shoes?"

She wrinkled her nose. "Yes, but…" She almost hadn't, but had feared her feet swelling on the airplane.

He lifted an eyebrow and waited silently.

She couldn't help herself. "They're ugly, okay? I only bought them last year when my brother stepped on my toe with his heavy cop shoes and broke it."

He held up his hand. "I promise not to think the less of you because you are wearing less-than-fashionable footwear. I have a nice collection of Italian leather shoes myself."

"I noticed your shoes when you came to my shop. I admire good footwear in a man."

"How lucky for me." He pulled her close. "I also have many excellent suits, Egyptian cotton shirts and Vinciguerra's largest collection of ties." He nuzzled her neck. "As you well know, they are sewn of finest silk that slips over your skin yet still holds a firm knot. Perhaps you would like a closer look at them."

She glanced over her shoulder at the bedroom and gulped. The idea of him tying her hand and foot to the bed was wildly arousing, to put it mildly. She wet her lips and he groaned. "Enough. We need some fresh air." He turned her away from him. "Go put on your walking shoes. I promise I won't tell anyone."

Renata dug down to the bottom of her suitcase and pulled out the boxy white leather sneakers and a pair of white ankle socks. Her feet settled into the unaccustomed padding and actually felt good.

Not that she would wear gym shoes with her work clothing like a suburban commuter, but maybe on weekends…

"All right, here I am."

"Lovely. Now I don't have to worry about your twisting an ankle. The path to Corniglia can be steep."

"Corniglia? We're walking to Corniglia?" He had to be kidding. From what she'd seen on their boat trip, Corniglia was straight up a cliff. She'd even wondered in amazement that the whole town hadn't plunged into the Mediterranean drink aeons ago.

"You cannot come to Cinque Terre and not go to your ancestral village. It would be a terrible disgrace."

"But that sucker is vertical. They probably have to bring supplies in by rope and pulley," she whined.

He was implacable, and Renata shortly found herself wearing a floppy sun hat and carrying a backpack filled with sunblock, water and snacks. Giorgio wore matching gear but of course he didn't react to the sun like she did. He was even more of a bronzed god after a few days of sun exposure.

"All right, where to?"

"The trail starts up by the train station." He grabbed her hand and guided her toward the top of the town.

"No train going up there?" she asked wistfully.

"Not for us."

She gave up, but not before one last parting shot as they

started uphill. "If all my muscles cramp up, you're carrying me on your back."

He laughed. "Come on, city girl. You should see the hills in Vinciguerra."

"So that's why you have such nice legs." She leered at his strong calf muscles and tight glutes.

"Stop buttering me up and walk."

The trail wound around the base of the watchtower of what used to be the castle. It had crumbled away over the years and now was just a stretch of grass overlooking the harbor.

The watchtower was still impressive—perfectly round and made of dark gray, flat, rectangular stone. "The lookout for when Turkish and North African pirates came raiding for slaves in the Middle Ages. They would build fires to warn the other villages along the coasts."

Renata shivered. To be living in a sleepy Italian village where you never went anywhere else or met anyone else, and then to be kidnapped and sold into slavery in a Middle Eastern slave market. It was a horrifying thought. "Did they ever go home?"

"Some of them." He gave her a gentle smile. "Others would have adapted as best as they could to a new life."

She snorted. "You would have been bought by a lonely old widow and kept in the male version of the harem."

"As long as there was a sexy redheaded maidservant who could sneak in, I would be content." He wrapped his arm around her waist. "Now come—let me take your picture. How about there?" Giorgio pointed to a section of trail with a great view of the harbor.

"Okay." She faced him and smiled as he took several pictures.

"That looks great with the boats behind you."

A young couple came around the corner and oohed and ahhed at the view. They spotted Giorgio and Renata.

"Hey, y'all speak English?" the pretty blonde woman asked. Her dark-haired boyfriend wore a University of Texas shirt, so no bonus points for guessing where they were from.

Not quite like she did, but close enough. "Sure, I'm from New York."

Apparently, from the amused glance between them, her accent was just as entertaining. Giorgio didn't say anything.

"This is such a super spot—we could take y'all's picture and then if you didn't mind, you could take ours," the woman offered.

"Oh, sure. You want to go first?"

The blonde handed her a pink cell phone. "Sure! Chase and I are on our honeymoon…" She stopped to gaze adoringly at Texas Longhorn Man. "And we're updating our Facebook as we go."

"Every ten minutes, Mandy?" the groom grumbled.

The happy couple posed in front of the Vernazza harbor and Renata fired off several shots, feeling rather like a prom photographer when Mandy turned Chase so she could gaze into his eyes and looped her arms around his neck as if they were slow dancing.

"Thanks!" Mandy bounded back up toward them. "Now your turn!" She accepted Giorgio's camera. Renata decided to hang on to Mandy's pink one so she couldn't accidentally take Giorgio's photo and plaster it on her Facebook wall.

"Come on, George, let's get our picture taken." Renata thought she heard Giorgio sigh but he followed her to the scenic spot.

He slipped his arm around her waist. "All right, *Renée*." She winced. She'd been mistakenly called that since she was a kid.

"Snuggle in so I can get a great shot." Mandy aimed Giorgio's digital camera and took a few pictures. "How romantic! Don't they look sweet together, honey-bun?"

Chase grunted, either in agreement or disgust at being called "honey-bun" in public. Renata wasn't sure which.

Giorgio was shaking with silent laughter by then. "Do not ever call me 'honey-bun,'" he muttered.

"Don't worry," she spoke out of the corner of her mouth. "I'd wear black socks with tennis shoes before I do that."

Mandy finished, and she and Renata traded equipment. "It's so neat to meet other honeymooners, isn't it, Chase? We're staying in Manarolo at the cute little hotel above the Dionysus wine bar, so stop by if you want to hang out."

"Thank you." Giorgio gave her his most gracious nod, turning his green gaze full wattage on her. "Have a wonderful time here in Cinque Terre."

"Oh, my." She stared up at him in wonder. "You have the cutest accent, doesn't he, Chase?"

Chase was understandably less enthused. "Him and every other guy here in Italy."

Sensing a potential brouhaha in Honeymoon-Land, Renata pulled Giorgio down the trail. "Congrats! Happy honeymoon!" she called over her shoulder.

He hurried after her. "Ah, Texans certainly are friendly. I expect meeting fellow honeymooners George and Renée will make her next posting. If only you New Yorkers were as easygoing."

"Hey, we have things to do—we can't run around after cattle all day."

He laughed. "I'd pay a thousand euros to see you in cowboy boots running after a cow. Red boots, to match your hair."

She groaned. "I barely do hiking trails—I definitely do not do cow pastures."

"How do you do with vineyards?"

"Can I get some wine?"

"Once we get to the top," he promised.

She took a deep breath. Never let it be said New York girls lacked grit. "Let's go."

The trail was steep but green with lush vineyards, and despite Giorgio's initial whip-cracking, he stopped often to admire the scenery and gallantly ignored the loud wheezing noises emanating from her lungs. They hit a wider point on the trail next to a nasty-looking cactus plant.

"Wow, I didn't know it was warm enough for cactuses up here."

A grizzled old vineyard worker came over to greet them. He and Giorgio chatted in Italian. "Ah." Giorgio nodded. "He says these are called *fichi d'india*—figs from India. I think the English name for them is prickly pear cactus fruit. I had some in California once."

The old guy told Giorgio something else.

"He says he is sorry you are not here in late summer. They are a beautiful golden-yellow and so sweet and juicy. You will have to return to try them. He promises you will love them."

Giorgio gestured to Renata and told him that her ancestors came from Corniglia, which inspired an excited exchange.

"He said, of course you are from Corniglia because you are a beautiful girl and everyone knows the girls from Corniglia are the most beautiful in Italy. I told him the most beautiful in Europe."

"Aww." She smiled up at him.

"Well, anyway…" Giorgio reddened slightly under his tan. "He says to visit his cousin's wine shop on the main square and tell him Carlo sent us."

"Sounds great. And maybe something to eat."

"Of course." They shook hands all around and headed uphill again. "Carlo also said we passed the nudist beach a while back."

"Really? I don't remember that."

"No, I didn't see any nudists, either. It must not be nudist tourist season yet."

Renata shuddered at the idea of full-frontal sunbathing. All the money in the world couldn't make her risk sun-burned breasts and even worse…a sunburned…no, that would never happen.

"Carlo said that back in the seventies, the locals, not being fond of nudist tourists, stormed the main beach and gave them the boot to that smaller beach farther away."

"Tourists without anywhere to carry their wallets are never welcome," she informed him.

"Apparently the national park service may buy the cur-rent beach and kick them out again."

"Oh, those poor nudists. Whatever will they do?"

"Go to one of several hundred other clothing-optional beaches around the Mediterranean." He shrugged. "I know you Americans think they are full of centerfold models, but really, they are not that interesting. Imagine people your parents' age, your grandparents' age, lying naked on towels and you can see how it is very far from arousing."

Renata made a horrified face. "I'm gonna have to drink a *lot* of Corniglian wine to get that image out of my head."

"Poor, sheltered girl." He grabbed her hand to help her up a particularly narrow stretch of trail. "Let's go get you some wine."

A while later, Renata straggled into Corniglia. "This is so pretty." A wide town square with some sort of war me-morial in the middle overlooked an old stone church and that all-important Italian village institution, the soccer field. A bright yellow school building stood to their left, and she realized it had been turned into a hostel. Right now, she just wanted to get off her feet. "Let's find Carlo's cousin." Sensible shoes or no, the dogs were barking.

"You did a good job." Giorgio pulled her in close and kissed her. "As a special treat, we will take the train back."

She sagged against him. "Oh, thank goodness."

They found a table at the local wine bar in the main square, the Largo Taragio, under the shadow of an ancient gray-and-white stone church. It looked almost like a bird-house with its round dark window above a tall narrow pair of dark doors. A curiously modern verdigris bronze statue of a boy looked over the square. Renata tried to figure out what he was supposed to be and gave up under the mental strain.

Giorgio quickly ordered a bottle of water, a bottle of the famous local white wine and the fixed-menu lunch for both of them. Renata closed her eyes and drank a glass of water. "Ah, that tastes good." She picked up her wineglass and sniffed the fresh aroma. "But that will taste better." Had her ancestors made similar wine? Maybe even using fruit from the same vines, since the plants could live hundreds of years.

Giorgio raised his own glass. "To Renata—on this very special occasion of her return to Corniglia."

She leaned over to kiss him. "Thank you, Giorgio. That was lovely."

"This visit, everything, has always been for you. I want you to remember this day always."

"I will," she promised. Every day with Giorgio would be burned into her memory.

The waiter quickly brought them an *antipasto misto,* a mixed appetizer plate consisting of delicious mussels stuffed with buttered breadcrumbs and saffron, sweet prawns in lemon juice and a ringlike dish that Renata couldn't quite identify.

Giorgio asked the waiter. "He says it is *una insalata,* a chilled squid salad with olives and tomatoes."

"Really." She jabbed one of the rings, and boy, the tines of her fork bounced back like she'd poked a rubber ball.

"Do you dare?" he teased her.

"What the hell," she muttered, forking a tentacle segment into her mouth. Couldn't be that much different from octopus, could it?

Several minutes of chewing later, she realized cold squid was a bit tougher to eat than warm, cooked octopus. At least it was tasty, the olives, superfresh tomatoes and hint of capers and oregano jazzing it up.

She abandoned the squid when her pasta came, a mix of steamed mussels, clams and prawns tossed in a tomato-parsley sauce.

Giorgio went for the local fresh anchovies over pasta. "Want one?" He offered her one of the tiny fish.

She accepted, eating it with gusto. "I can't believe I'm eating anchovies. My brothers would laugh their asses off if they saw me. I used to gag when they'd get them on a pizza."

"Ah, but this was swimming in the sea last night. Those that make it to New York are processed in unmentionable ways before they are shipped—mashed into a tin can and handled roughly."

"Ah, kind of like my flight out of Genoa the day after tomorrow." She meant it as a joke but it came out flat. That was the one topic they had avoided discussing—her leaving.

He cleared his throat. "Yes, I have had flights like that." He changed the subject back to food and she went along with him, not wanting to spoil their afternoon, either.

They passed on a main course but Renata couldn't resist the homemade gelato, flavored with honey from local bees. It was so creamy and sweet she had a hard time resisting the urge to lick out the bowl. Giorgio didn't order any dessert but consented to her feeding him a couple spoonfuls.

After finishing her dish, she leaned back in her chair. "Listen, Giorgio, I won't need a train ticket. You can just roll me down the hill."

"No rolling. Time to walk it off." He left money for the tab and pulled her to her feet.

Despite his threat to walk off her lunch, he set a leisurely pace hand in hand through the town, stopping to peer into various small shops. They also strolled into the surprisingly bright birdhouse church, which was actually something called the Oratory of St. Catherine, a meeting place for various Catholic groups in the village, but not specifically a church.

The ceiling above the white-and-gold altar was painted a cool sky blue with white clouds. Right below the main dome was a large round oil painting of a cheerful woman sitting on a green throne and surrounded by fat blond cherubs. Presumably St. Catherine, if her memories from Catholic school didn't fail her.

Just standing in the not-quite-a-church took some of the buzzing thoughts out of her head. She would figure out what to do about her growing feelings for Giorgio later. They had each other for the time being, and she wouldn't sandbag her last couple days with worry.

She sighed out a big breath of relief. Giorgio looked down curiously at her. "Are you all right?"

She smiled up at him. "Great. Now this is art, isn't it?"

He laughed, obviously remembering the barbed wire and cornstalk mess that passed for art in some circles. "It's beautiful. We have a similar chapel in Vinciguerra. My ancestor built it in penance for sacking a neighboring principality. Unfortunately that prince was the Pope's cousin."

"Oops!" Feudal Europe certainly had been a different world.

"Yes, that particular ancestor was more a man of action than a man of thought. And he kept half of what he had looted, figuring the other prince got off lightly."

"And in the meantime, my ancestors were making wine in their huts and trying to avoid being sold in a Turkish slave market. That is, if the slavers could even make it up the hill without collapsing."

"Probably easier to go elsewhere, I imagine." They drifted out of the oratory and around the village. Renata tried to imagine living here all her life, marrying a local boy and raising a crop of kids along with the grapes.

There was something about Italy that made her think of fertility. The fruit of the land, the fish in the sea, the bright sky. She sneaked a look at Giorgio. And of course, Mr. Sex God in person. Everything about him spoke of potency and reproduction. He would make some beautiful babies, dark-haired with pretty green eyes. A little girl with beautiful black curls that would look great with a gold satin headband...

Whoa. That was a weird thought. Yes, of course she knew the connection between sex and babies, but aside from an occasional chill down her spine, the idea of small, adorable children did not cross her mind at all.

Was she looking at Giorgio as a possible baby-maker? She stopped dead in her tracks. So did he. "Are you all right?"

Hell, no! She'd taken the batteries out of her biological clock as soon as she hit puberty. That sucker had never ticked in her life. It wouldn't start now. Would it?

"Renata?" He gently brushed a sweaty lock of hair off her face as if she were all fancied up for a formal ball.

She stared at him. "Yes, yes, I'm fine. Maybe a bit thirsty."

"We'll find a drink for you. How about a bottle of lemonade?"

"Sounds good." She shoved her disturbing thoughts deep down and smiled. "Lead the way as we sack Corniglia for its lemonade."

14

THE NEXT DAY, Renata had only dressed and made it out to the terrace after a couple pain relievers, a hot shower that strained the goodwill of an Italian water heater and two pastries with coffee. Giorgio had offered to give her a massage, but she had put him off until later when she could hopefully enjoy it more.

Giorgio had gone out to check if her packet of sample Italian fabrics and laces had arrived from his assistant yet, so Renata had some time to laze around the apartment on her own.

She was enjoying an Italian soap opera that seemed to involve evil twins, secret babies and husbands returning from the dead when her phone rang. She answered it. "Hey, Flick."

"Hey, yourself. How goes sunny Italy?"

"It's going, going, gone—just like me the day after tomorrow."

"Well, yeah. All vacations come to an end. Otherwise we'd be living on the beach in a cardboard box."

Renata grunted.

"Don't bail on me now, Renata. I've been smiling at these brides so long my mouth's dried out. Any more time here and I'll have to grease my teeth with Vaseline like those Amazon beauty queens."

That momentarily distracted her. "Really? That's what they do in beauty pageants?"

"Gross, isn't it? I saw it on the reality TV channel. They also use double-stick tape to keep their dresses and swimsuits in place."

"Holy crap. I would think a flash of skin would get extra points."

"A wardrobe malfunction is a dangerous thing, Renata. It's been known to topple entire civilizations."

They both had a good laugh, but Renata quickly fell silent.

"Aren't you going to ask me how your precious business is doing while you bop your brains out?"

"How is my business doing?" she asked dutifully, but her heart wasn't in it. How nuts was that? She'd worked eighty-hour weeks the past several years to make it a raging hipster success and now she couldn't even remember to ask about it.

"You don't want to come back, do you?"

"What? That's crazy. Why wouldn't I want to come back to New York? Everything important is there, after all." Not Giorgio, though.

"Not your prince," Flick uncannily echoed her thoughts.

"His sister lives there. He'll be in New York sometimes."

"If they're planning a big hometown wedding, it'll be more likely for her to go back to Vinciguerra to work on things instead."

"Oh. I guess." She'd never considered that possibility, and it was an unpleasant one. "Wow. Well…" Her eyes started to fill and she brushed them with displeased amazement. Really…what was wrong with her?

Flick, perceptive as she was, had an answer. "Babe, I

hate to be the one to tell you this, but you know what I think?"

"What?" Renata forced out between dry lips.

Flick cleared her throat, her usually flip mood totally absent. "I think you went and fell in love with the guy, Renata."

"No," her mouth said, while her head and her heart said *Nyah, nyah, yes, you did!* "No," she repeated loudly. "No, I didn't! People don't fall in love like this after only a week. This is a vacation fling. The real world doesn't come into play. I came to Italy for a lighthearted, fun vacation and, dammit, I am having lighthearted fricking fun!" She realized she was shouting absurdities into the phone but couldn't help herself.

"Okay, okay," Flick said soothingly as if Renata were the crazy lady who lived in a box across from their subway stop and was starting to see purple aliens pop up from the sidewalk. "You're right. Of course you're right. Nobody falls in love like that. It takes weeks, months, years. Hell, some people never fall in love—like you and me, right, Renata?"

"That's right, Flick!"

Flick blew out a loud sigh that she probably didn't mean to carry quite so well over the phone lines. Great, Flick thought she was a basket case and was probably already blocking out time in her schedule to buy wine—non-Italian, of course—to commiserate with her as she bawled into her wine, and then hold her hair back as she barfed up her overindulgence in wine. And a good time was had by all—not!

Renata took a deep breath. Her mental whine/wine sce-
~io was frighteningly possible. And why would that be?
~erchance, would a former Goth girl turned hard-

nosed New York entrepreneur need alcohol and sympathy on her parting from a guy she'd only met eight days earlier?

Because she'd fallen in love with the jerk! "Shit."

"What?" Flick asked cautiously.

"You know damn well," she said crossly. "I did. I did go and fall in love with him." Her stomach churned. "I think I'm going to puke." How stupid could she have been? She flopped back onto the bed and banged her head on the pillows a couple times.

"Renata, are you there?"

"Yeah," she muttered sullenly.

"If it makes you feel any better…" Renata rolled her eyes. She'd never heard a good ending to a sentence that started with that phrase, but Flick continued bravely, "If it makes you feel any better, you really had the deck stacked against you. Your prince is good-looking, swept you off your feet to a wonderful seaside resort and is fabulous in the sack from what I can read between the lines, since you never did tell me the really good parts, Renata!" Flick sounded pissed for a second and then laughed. "That should have been a clue right there for you."

"What?"

"You didn't want to spill any details because you were starting to care for him and didn't want to giggle with me over your sweet lovin'."

"Don't be silly. That doesn't mean anything."

"Okay, what position does he like best? How big does he get? What's his personal record for rocking your world?"

Renata clamped her lips together before she realized what she was doing.

"Oh, ho, ho!" Flick crowed. "I never got one good story out of you—not even from the first day you met, and I bet that was a doozy."

She couldn't help grinning at her memory of a certain

limo ride. "But wait—does that mean I loved him even then?"

"Love at first sight—who ever heard of such a thing? Oh, yeah, every single goober who ever wrote any poem about love."

Renata's eyes began to sting and she bit her lip. "Promise me you won't tell him, Flick."

"You think I'd rat you out? Call up the Royal Palace in Vinciguerra and leave a message with his secretary?"

"No, of course not."

"You need to rat yourself out."

"What?" Renata jumped to her feet. "Tell him? Oh, no, oh, no."

"Oh, yes, oh, yes. Tell the man how you feel and you too can be saying that, only under much pleasanter conditions."

Renata clutched the phone and sank back onto the chair. "Flick, he's a *prince*. I'm a dress designer."

"Hey, it worked pretty well for Cinderella, didn't it? And besides, what are you, a stupid peasant girl, bowing down before royalty? Or are you a strong, Italian-American girl from Brooklyn who bows to no one? Grow a pair and tell him how you feel."

Renata sat up straight. "Yeah. But what if he says, 'I'm flattered but here's your ticket back to New York'?"

She sighed. "Do I have to spell out everything? Then say thanks for the trip and come home, Renata. Sheesh. I think you've been out in the sun too long."

"Oh, Flick."

"Go on. Stop whining to me and move it. Where did Prince Charming go, anyway?"

"He said he had to run some errands, so he just left a few minutes ago."

"Go after him, Renata."

Renata jumped to her feet. "Chase after a man? I have my pride."

"Great. I'll see you at the airport tomorrow. Be sure to pack up your pride nice and snug so the baggage handlers don't damage it on your return trip."

Renata grimaced. Flick was right, dammit. She'd never been a coward, and it was embarrassing to admit she might chicken out. "All right, Flick. Off I go. There's only a small shopping area so I can find him easily."

"Get going. Text me when you can."

A CROWD WAS GATHERED around the newsstand talking excitedly and waving their hands. Renata craned her neck to see what was going on. Had someone been caught passing off bad fish? Did the local team lose a major soccer match? Had Italy declared war against Vinciguerra?

Renata didn't really care, but an older woman at the edge of the crowd spotted her and jabbed her neighbor in the ribs, both falling silent. A few more jabbed ribs and quickly hushed conversations, and the whole crowd of locals was staring at her.

"Ah. *Buon giorno.*" She waved awkwardly at them. Maybe the cat was out of the bag about Giorgio's celebrity status and she was being eyeballed as the companion *du jour.* Well, fair enough. It was none of their business anyway.

One of the older gents pointed at her and said loudly, *"Si, è lei."*

Yes, it's her? Renata looked around but she was the only one standing there.

As if by some prearranged signal, the crowd parted and she saw a rack of garish-looking tabloids. Her stomach flipped as she slowly approached the rags, her knees stiff.

No way! The Italian *and* the British ones both had front page shots of Giorgio as he'd swum with the dolphins.

Judging from the angle, probably one of those sailors had taken the photos. If she found out which one, she'd toss him overboard and let the fish nibble him to death.

So why did the locals recognize her? She picked up the British one, even tackier than American tabloids if that were possible, and flipped to the inside story.

Yep, there she was climbing up the boat ladder, wet red hair and white bikini with the cherries looking like polka dots.

She forced her eyes to read the text. Usual stuff about sexy prince and mysterious redhead frolicking in the sunny Italian Riviera, etc, etc. Thankfully she was too pasty to go topless and they hadn't gotten any shots while she and Giorgio "frolicked" on the apartment terrace.

But then—now her stomach was really cramping—the part she hadn't known.

Prince Giorgio of Vinciguerra is lucky to be cavorting in the sea after a recent fright for his life at a New York hospital. According to insiders at Manhattan Medical Center, the bachelor prince arrived suffering chest pains.

Chest pains?" she muttered. Giorgio acted as healthy as a horse.

Renata read further.

Too much work and not enough play was the diagnosis. The prescription? Rest and relaxation, and it seems the magnificent monarch has found both in the arms—and charms—of his sexy redheaded gal pal.

She wrinkled up her mouth. "'Gal pal,' my ass." And what was that crap about a prescription for R & R? She'd known he'd needed a vacation, but it had been medically necessary?

"Signorina?" the old lady running the newsstand asked cautiously. Renata could feel a flush creeping up her neck.

"Here." She tossed a handful of euros onto the counter and took a copy of each colorful publication. She spun on her heel and stalked back to their apartment, the villagers watching her with wide eyes.

She crashed the door open. "Giorgio!"

"Ah, Renata." He came toward her with open arms, slowly dropping them to his side as she clutched the tabloids to her chest. "What is wrong? What do you have there?"

She shook the papers at him. "One of those sailors sold photos of us to this British magazine. And this Italian one, too, although I couldn't read the story. God only knows what *that* one says."

"Renata *mia,* I am so sorry. I thought we might avoid their notice by coming to such a small town before the busy season started."

"That's not the point. Read the article." She shoved the British one at him.

He read the article, his face darkening.

"Is that true? You went to the emergency room with chest pains?" Her own chest hurt at the thought of what must have been his pain and fear.

"Yes. Yes, I did."

"When?"

For the first time, he looked embarrassed and unsure of himself. "The day we met."

"Before or after we met?"

"After," he admitted.

Her eyebrows shot up into her hair. "So after our wonderful day in New York and some heavy-duty stuff at night, you dropped me off and Paolo rushed you to the emergency room."

"Yes."

"With chest pains."

"Yes. But not a heart attack, fortunately."

"Fortunately," she echoed. "So what was it?"

"Chili dogs."

"Indigestion? And anything else?" She wanted to see if the tabloid report of his overwork and stress was true.

"Not really."

"Why did you go to the E.R.? Certainly you've had indigestion before?"

"Paolo was worried."

"And after you left the E.R., you called me to invite me to Italy with you. Were you even home by then or did you call me from the car?"

He shifted. "The car."

She was getting mighty sick of his short answers. "Giorgio, something's not adding up here. God knows these magazines are not the fount of truth, but they say the E.R. doc told you the chest pains were partly caused by too much work and not enough play."

He winced again. "Renata, I am a busy man. I do have much work and I haven't had a vacation in several years."

"That's not what I mean!" She threw the papers on the floor. "We met and had a great time. Then you decided to invite me to Italy to blow off some steam and I accepted because we really hit it off. But I'm missing something here. You never told me anything about your hospital trip. You never said the doctors told you to take it easy. That's why you wouldn't eat much bread or pasta, right? They even put you on a diet." She started to tear up. "We never took it easy. All that hiking, swimming and sex. I could have killed you."

"Ah, but what a way to go." He gave her a devilish grin.

"Jerk!"

He looked confused. "The doctor never told me not to have sex."

"Not that, *stupido!* You lied to get me here to Italy. You never mentioned any of this medical crisis. I thought you wanted me here so we could spend time with each other, have some fun..." *Fall in love.* She angrily brushed away that thought.

"I regret my actions have caused you distress."

"Ah." She stared at him, but he didn't say anything more. And why did he need to explain anything to her?

He never pretended to be someone he wasn't, had never spoken of undying love for her in an attempt to get her in the sack. But something wasn't jibing. Even if he had told her ninety-nine percent of the truth, he was still hiding something. She could read it in the way he had put on his formal manners instead of just being plain Giorgio, the man she had come to care for over the past week. "What else is going on, Giorgio?"

"Nothing." His face closed down, his expression as lively as an emperor's profile carved on an ancient coin.

She narrowed her eyes. "I may only be a dressmaker from the backstreets of Brooklyn but I know when some guy is blowing smoke up my skirt."

"I am not, as you say, blowing smoke anywhere. I wanted to be with you and took the opportunity to invite you here. Do you regret coming?"

She stared at him. How could she answer that? She'd loved every minute she spent with him, both in New York and Italy. That was the problem. The more time she spent with him, the more she longed for him—and the less she wanted to leave him. "I...I don't know."

He grew even more remote. "I see."

No, he didn't, but telling him she had done something incredibly stupid like fall in love with him would make things even more awkward and awful. "I need to get back to New York." That was part of the truth. "My business needs me, and I'm sure your country needs you." She sounded like a military recruiting poster. Vinciguerra needs *You,* Prince Giorgio.

"Yes, of course." He pulled his phone off his belt clip with a smooth move. She hid her trembling hands in the folds of her skirt. He tapped a few commands into his phone. "I've changed your flight to an earlier one. Paolo will make arrangements with Captain Galletti to get you to Genoa in plenty of time. You can leave within the hour."

Her nails bit into her palms. "Fine. Good. I will go pack."

He gave her a brusque nod. "I will leave you to it. In the meantime, I need to run an errand." He replaced his phone and disappeared out the door.

Renata swallowed hard, a bitter taste in her mouth. Was he even bothering to come back to say goodbye or was it another of Paolo's job requirements to clean up messy romantic entanglements, as well?

She looked at the clock over the small dining table. Well, screw Prince Giorgio and his minion. She'd get her own butt back to Genoa and they could take a flying leap. Spinning on her heel, she blew through the bedroom and bath, stuffing her belongings willy-nilly into a suitcase. Forget the bottles of Scciachetrà, forget the frilly lingerie. The wine would sour in her stomach and the sight of the undergarments would make her cry. If she had time, she'd burn them in the outdoor fireplace, but she didn't.

All Renata wanted to do was to get home to New York, where she could make wedding dresses for girls stupid enough to believe in happy endings. There would be none for her.

GIORGIO KNEW HIS LEGS were moving because he was descending, but the rest of him was numb. He arrived at the street level somehow and his feet slowly picked a path along the cobbled streets.

Renata was leaving him, going back to her real life in New York City. She hadn't told him never to call her again, but she hadn't left the door open for him, either, telling him she partially regretted coming to Italy with him.

What had he done that was so terrible she had to leave him even sooner than anticipated? He had given her a fairy-tale vacation, complete with seaside cruise, romantic hikes and a cozy villa for their lovemaking.

Images of her face lit with passion flashed to his mind and his breath left him with a whoosh. She had been like no other woman—and no other would ever measure up to her.

He stared at the brightly painted houses and shops. He knew he would never return to Vernazza, could never stand to return to the Cinque Terre again in his life. The café where they ate breakfast, the trattoria where they ate dinner. The gift store where she'd bought the inexpensive souvenirs for her family. And the lingerie store with a sheer, flowing nightgown in the window. He stumbled slightly on a raised stone and caught himself before falling.

The worst thing is that he probably would have to see Renata again in the course of the wedding events. It was not unusual for designers to help the bride dress for the wedding ceremony in case of last-minute mishaps or alterations.

If he told Stevie the truth about what had happened between Renata and him, she would cancel her gown out of misguided loyalty, the gown that she loved and that made her look like an angel descending to earth. All three of them could be miserable: him for losing Renata, Renata for losing her commission and Stevie for losing her gown.

Hopefully by then the pain of missing her would lessen from the current hot coal sitting in his chest. If he hadn't recently been assured of at least marginal good health in that aspect, he would have sworn his heart was literally breaking.

Again memories of her threatened to flood his self-control. Renata giving him the eye as she flirted with him in her shop. Renata sleeping so innocently tangled up in their sheets. Renata laughing with the dolphins.

Giorgio stopped at the window of a small jewelry store. Diamonds, rubies, gold and platinum. None shone as bright as she did.

If only he were plain George di Leone, New York businessman. He would date Renata for the minimally acceptable amount of time, give her a diamond ring and then have her design the most beautiful gown in the world for the most beautiful bride.

If only.

But no, he was Prince Giorgio, ruler of his very own country in the back reaches of the Italian peninsula. What woman would want to give up her New York address, her New York business for a position, royal though it may be, that sucked away most of your privacy and tied you to duty for the good part of your life?

There would have to be a very good reason. Giorgio stopped in his tracks. He knew her well enough to know that riches and power would never sway her, not even the most expensive item in the jewelry store.

He saw a small heart-shaped pendant made of diamonds. That heart. Her heart. His heart. His heart that he worried about so, worried at every minor twinge—he worried about it stopping when he should have been worried about it breaking.

He pressed a hand to his chest. It thumped strongly, but for what? An empty heart could live a long time, but for what? No Renata to listen to it as she rested in his arms, no Renata to fill it with her smiles and her…love?

It was almost a blow, that realization. Was she so upset because she loved him?

A gasp escaped his lips. And he had done what to deserve her love? Nothing. In fact, he had kicked it away like a football in a World Cup tournament.

Moron! He clenched his fist. He needed to find her. Would she believe him…believe that he loved her? Because he did. How would he convince her?

By giving her this heart of his, this unquenchable burning that she had set aflame since the first smile of her ruby lips. It was the only thing he had to offer her that she might accept.

He immediately ran back to the villa, cursing his previous stupidity with every step. How had he not realized he loved her?

He arrived at the stairs leading up and stopped short. Instead of a beautiful redhead waiting for him to come to his senses, Paolo stood there.

"Where? Where is she?" He pushed past Paolo, but his driver put a beefy hand on his shoulder.

"*Signore,* she is gone before I get here."

"Gone? How?" He searched wildly up and down the street.

Paolo jerked his head up the hill. "I think she must have taken the train. It left only a few minutes ago—the train to Genoa."

He clutched at his head. "Paolo, I love her. I can't stand to lose her. What do I do?"

"Cancel her plane ticket."

Always the practical one. "Right." He grabbed his phone and called the airline, his face contorting as he listened to the ticket agent. He hung up. "Paolo, she already canceled her ticket and bought herself a new one—I can't cancel that." Renata and her stubborn pride. He didn't know whether to admire or curse her independence.

"Capitano Galletti is waiting for us at the dock. We can intercept her before she gets to Genoa."

Giorgio was already running. "Let's go." He'd already made a terrible mistake by letting her go once—he wouldn't make that mistake twice.

RENATA STARED GLASSY-EYED out the window of the train as it jolted along the tracks. All she had to do was get to the airport, get on the plane and then get home. Once she was back in New York, she could fall apart, cry all she wanted and generally act like a lovelorn maniac without involving airport security, customs or Interpol.

She had passed the point of beating herself up for falling in love with Giorgio and was just trying to numb herself for the next several hours. Would several airport cocktails help with that or turn her into a sniveling mess? Hard to say. She tried but failed to suppress a sigh.

The older woman sitting next to her took that as a signal to chat. She offered her a strawberry, delicious and fresh from her garden.

Renata shook her head and told her no thank you. She would choke if she tried to swallow anything.

"*Signorina,* you sick?" Her seatmate furrowed her sun-weathered brow. Her eyes were dark and kind, her graying hair pulled back into a bun. She was the quintessential Italian mamma, and that made Renata feel even more homesick.

"No, um, sad." Her tears started to well up despite her

efforts at ice-maidenhood. Damn that Giorgio! For someone so wonderful, he sure was making her miserable.

"Oh, bad. *La famiglia sta bene?*"

"Yes, my family is fine. A man—*un uomo.*"

"Bah!" Her face lit up in knowing disgust. She turned
to the other women and explained Renata's distress, wrapping a heavy, comforting arm around her shoulder.

A white-haired woman with the face of a dried apple
waved her hands. "Pah!" She spit on the train's floor and
shook her head. The other women made noises of sympathy.

Her new friend patted her hand with her work-roughened
one. "*Si,* you find new man. A girl so *bella*—easy. *Bella
figura, bella faccia.* The men all chase you. My son—he
very 'ansome. He own a boat for fish," she said enticingly.

Renata smiled politely. Even a fisherman who probably
lived with his mamma sounded better than Giorgio.

The train slowed to a stop. From the loud protests and
big gestures, it wasn't a planned stop. Hmm, who had the
clout to stop a train? It had better be some stray animal on
the tracks, or else.

The women were worked up into a frenzied pitch by
the time the door slid open and the conductor came in. He
cringed at the noisy imprecations and protests aimed his
way. Making a placating gesture, he stepped to the side and
there *he* was.

Renata groaned and jumped to her feet. "Get lost, Giorgio!"

He extended a hand to her. "Renata, please. Listen to
me."

"You aren't the boss here—this isn't even your country."

Her seatmate turned her glare to Giorgio. "He the man
you cry for?"

Renata turned her puffy, sore gaze at him. "Yes."

"Oh, Renata." Giorgio's face sagged and he tried to say something to her.

Renata's new protectress shouted something to the other women and in the blink of an eye, she pulled a ripe tomato from her sack.

"Wait, no…" Renata tugged at the woman's arm but she shook her off and chucked it straight at him.

That was the signal to the other women and Giorgio's immaculate white linen shirt soon looked like the canvas of a Jackson Pollock splatter painting. He twisted and tried to get out of the way, but the railroad car was narrow and he was pinned down.

She gasped and laughed at the same time, but then the farm-fresh eggs came out. Even the hens were on her side in this female battle. "No more!" she shouted in Italian. "Enough!" Eggshells were sharp. She should know; she'd walked on them often enough.

The women grumbled and gave Giorgio the *malocchio,* the Italian version of the stink eye.

Giorgio wiped tomato pulp off his face and plucked an anchovy off his shoulder. "Your new friends certainly look after you, Renata."

"Yes, well…" She'd definitely won the pity vote on her unexpectedly short train ride. "What do you want, Giorgio?"

After a wary look around, he approached her. She stood, arms folded across her chest. "Renata, I want you—"

"Yeah, I already knew that." He wanted her, all right. Wanted her as the sexual equivalent of a stress reliever. "You could have told me the truth, you know. You could have said, 'Hey, Renata, I need a vacation or my doctor says I'll keel over. Feel like having sex with me in Italy? I'll find a nice hotel.'"

The women muttered angrily, getting the gist of her

accusation. She continued, "Instead, you have to go and lie and tell me all that crap about how you can't stop thinking of me."

"All of it true." He glanced warily at the women. "Please. Step outside with me for a minute—only a minute, I promise."

She pursed her lips but consented. Giorgio helped her down the train car's iron steps to a small stone terraced wall with grapevines dangling above it. "Please sit with me." He waited until she grudgingly sat, a good foot and a half away from him.

"I don't even want to look at you," she informed him, not quite telling the truth. He was so beautiful he made her eyes hurt, even with the equivalent of a spaghetti dinner for five on his shirt.

"Don't, then. Listen to me."

She fought a quivering lip but nodded.

"Renata, I am sorry."

She made a hurry-it-up motion with her hand. He already said that and she still didn't believe him.

"I know you are hurt and I would give anything to prevent that. The magazine article, part of it is true. I was in the hospital after that chili dog and I thought it was a heart attack."

"Why? You're so young."

"My father, I told you how he and my mother died in a car accident in Vinciguerra when I was just starting at the university."

"Yes." She hoped he wasn't aiming for sympathy, cuz she was fresh out.

"My parents had gone away for a quiet weekend at the house in the country and were driving back to the city when my father had a massive heart attack. He dropped dead at the wheel. They were on a hilly road and the auto went over the edge of a ravine, landing about thirty meters down."

Renata whipped her head around in shock. He was as pale as his tan would let him be and his lips were bracketed in white lines. Oh, yes, he was telling her the truth now. "How terrible."

"My mother was of course alive at the time of impact and had severe internal and head injuries. Although they flew her to the trauma center immediately, they could do nothing for her and she died five days later."

Renata's eyes began to sting.

"So you see, that is how Stefania came to live with me. She was inconsolable in Vinciguerra and screamed for our mamma every night. My grandmother was afraid she would have a nervous breakdown so she sent Stevie to me in New York for a change of scenery. We were always close and I was the only one who could calm her."

Renata sniffled. Damn him, she did not want to feel one iota of sympathy for the man.

"When I thought I was having a heart attack, I thought of Stefania, of course. But I also thought of you."

"Me?"

"Yes, you. The woman I had only met that afternoon, the woman who was so kind to my sister, the woman who had made me crazy with her red lips and red hair and soft skin. I thought of you when I thought I was dying, and I bitterly regretted that I hadn't met you five years ago."

"Really?" Now her stinging eyes had decided to move directly to watery.

"Ten years ago. Forever ago." He dropped to his knees on the rocky ground and grabbed her hands. "Renata, *mia bella,* I don't want any more regrets. I have been entirely stupid but I am a poor, broken man without you." He took a deep breath. "I love you. *Ti amo,*" he repeated in Italian in case she hadn't gotten it the first time.

"Oh, Giorgio." She bit her lip.

"Tell me you feel the same," he pleaded, and he was not a man who pleaded. He mistook her hesitation for denial and his shoulders slumped. "I will not bother you any longer. If you do not want to take the train, I will have Paolo take you back to Genoa and get you a first-class ticket back to New York."

"Great, so I can sob my way back to the Big Apple like I was crying on the train? How considerate of you, Giorgio. First you tell me you love me, and then you want to get rid of me."

His head snapped up. "I do not want to be rid of you." He took a good look at her face. "It is your turn to tell the truth about how you feel, Renata. Don't be a sissy."

"A sissy? You think I'm a sissy because I haven't told you how much I love you?"

"You haven't," he goaded her. "I thought New Yorkers always spoke their minds. How much do you love me?"

"A ton. I fell in love with you days ago but was afraid—" Her lips turned downward as his turned up. Man, he'd tricked her not only into admitting she loved him but that she was scared about it. "I mean, I was…oh, all right, I love you, too, Giorgio. Now what the hell are we going to do?"

"We do what people in love do." His face split into a grin and he launched himself from his knees to wrap his arms around her. She shrieked as tomato pulp and fish guts smeared her clothing. "My shirt!" Her shriek was cut off by his kiss. It was a familiar kiss, but different, deeper, knowing the love behind it.

He finally lifted his head. "Now we are a matched set. I'll take you shopping for a new shirt anywhere you like."

"Oh, that's right—you're a prince. I forgot."

"Thank you for forgetting. For you, I am plain George di Leone, hapless brother of the bride."

"And don't forget, my love slave." She giggled, giddy.

"And you will be my princess."

She laughed. "Every Italian girl in New York is already a princess."

"No, Renata." Back to his knees again before she could blink. "Will you marry me and be my bride?"

She gaped at him. He was honest-to-God proposing to her? "Marry you?"

"*Si,* marry me. The prince and princess duties can be dull, but I apologize in advance. In important matters such as love, I am the same as any other man longing for his girl."

"Oh, no you're not. You are the sexiest, most wonderful man I've ever met. You're kind to your sister, loyal to your friends and I can't believe I met you." She impatiently swiped tears off her cheeks. She'd just cried in misery, now she was crying in joy? Her eyes were pink and her nose was red.

Fortunately Giorgio didn't care as he cupped her jaw in both hands, cradling her face as if she were a precious work of art. "I have been single for a long time and never met anyone like you. It is difficult for people to see beyond the trappings of my position and obligations to see the man. I always thought I would have plenty of time before I took my father's responsibilities, but that was not to be."

Renata caressed his hand, knowing the hole their deaths had left in his life.

"But I am not telling you this for pity. I want you to know that you will always be first for me—like my mother was for my father."

She didn't know what to say. The downside was immense. Become princess of Vinciguerra? Leave New York and her business and her family? "Giorgio, that's crazy. How long have we known each other? A week, that's how long. What will people think?"

He shook his head before she finished her protest. "Who cares? I am a grown man who knows his own mind. And don't tell me you care what other people think. I know you better than that." He kissed her nose and sat back, wrapping his arm around her waist.

She stared at him. Her life as a princess in Vinciguerra was almost unimaginable. But her life with Giorgio would be to wake up with him every morning, to kiss him every night, to watch his dark hair gradually lighten to gray, his green eyes undimmed by age.

A man she loved, who loved her back.

Oh, that would be enough upside for any woman.

His fingers tightened on her knee as he waited for her answer, tension radiating from him. She covered his hand with hers.

"Yes, Giorgio, I will marry you. I have no clue about this princess stuff but I do know about loving you and wanting to be with you forever." They'd work out the details later.

He crushed her into his tomatoed chest again, but his lips immediately distracted her, until her heart overflowed. She began to laugh at the wild improbability that her tough New York heart had been so easily turned to mush by a chivalrous Vinciguerran prince.

He lifted his mouth from hers and grinned, resting his forehead on hers. "We have a very interested audience."

Renata blinked slowly and turned her head toward the train. They sure did. Every single passenger was goggling at them from the windows, and her seatmate even stood on the metal steps for a better view. She gave a small sigh, but what did she expect, making out with a prince at the side of the railway?

"Ah, hello." She figured, what the hell, and sat up straight, giving them a wave to rival the Queen of England. "*Grazie!* Thank you for coming. You've been great! Read all about it in the next issue of *Today's Paparazzi!*"

Giorgio muffled a snort. "You are picking up on this very quickly."

The conductor approached them cautiously and Giorgio made quick arrangements to remove her suitcase. "For you will not go to Genoa today. I will come back to New York with you and meet your family, like a proper Vinciguerran man meets the family of his wife-to-be."

Hmm. Renata waited for the anticipated figure of Edvard Munch's *The Scream* to run across her mental landscape. Nope, the Italian birds were still chirping, the bright sun was still shining, and she had agreed to marry Giorgio Something Something Something di Leone. She didn't remember all his names. No more "Galaxy's Most Eligible Bachelor" for him. Maybe they could invite Mandy and Chase from Texas to their wedding. That would knock their socks off.

The train slowly pulled away, the passengers waving like crazy while some of the younger ones took their photos with their phones. Ah, well, welcome to life in the fishbowl.

She linked her arm with Giorgio's and carefully picked her way down the trail leading to where Paolo and the captain had anchored the boat. He was rock-steady, on the path and in her life. "You know, Giorgio, if we're going to have this big royal foo-foo wedding at some point, I'm going to have to remember your full name. I'd hate to look like a jerk on international television."

"Giorgio Alphonso Giuseppe Franco Martelli di Leone," he said slowly for her to catch all of his names.

"Good Lord, no wonder your friends call you George."

"*Si.*" He laughed. "But you may call me anything you

like, especially if it is 'my love,' *'amore mio,'* 'my heart,' *'mio cuore.'*"

She stopped. "And what will you call me?"

"The most wonderful woman in the world," he promptly answered. "The woman who has made my every dream come true, even when I did not know what I was dreaming for."

"Oh, Giorgio." She threw her arms around his waist and rested her head against his chest, her eyes filling again.

He set her suitcase down. "I know, I know. My heart is full, also."

"Just for a minute. Then we need to get down the hill so we can get out of these terrible clothes." The odor of tomatoes and anchovies was getting very strong.

He laughed, his chest rumbling under her ear. "Ah, I knew we were of like minds. You are a woman after my own heart."

She laughed and he joined in, her lighter giggles mixing with his warm masculine tones ringing through the countryside like a clear, strong bell announcing his joy. It was the finest, happiest sound she had ever heard, and joy welled in her, too.

A day of joy to start the rest of their joyful life together.

Epilogue

"I HAVE TO HAND IT TO YOU, George. How many men can go shopping for a wedding dress and wind up picking out a bride?" Frank's tone was admiring, after more than mild disbelief when Giorgio had called him from New York to announce his own engagement.

His face stretched into yet another love-struck grin. It was a good thing Frank couldn't see what had to be the most cow-eyed expression ever. "Not many, I suppose."

"You know, I went to the bridal salon when my sister got married." Frank definitely sounded disgruntled. "And do you know who was there? Women old enough to be my mother—my grandmother, even. Oh, and a couple flower girls who couldn't have been older than eight. But you, you find an Italian girl who looks like a redheaded Sophia Loren from that picture you emailed me. Where is the justice in the world?"

"There is none, Frank. I am amazed she's agreed to marry me."

"Me, too."

"Hey, you don't have to agree so quickly."

"Oh, knock off the false modesty, George. You know you're a great guy and I'm just kidding you. Tell me when the wedding is so I can dry-clean the formal wear."

"After Stefania's wedding. She deserves all the focus on her." Renata was definitely happy to leave the "big foo-foo royal wedding" to her sister-in-law to be.

"Don't get between a bride and her perfect day, eh? Good plan." Frank cleared his throat. "I heard from Jack. Not to rain on your parade, but he did pick up some bizarre ailment and they flew him to the hospital in Bangkok."

Giorgio winced. "Is he going to be all right?"

"Yes, yes," Frank soothed him. "Lost a few kilos he couldn't afford to lose but he claims he's much better."

"Frank, why doesn't he accept that professorship in tropical medicine they offered him at the Pasteur Institute last year?"

"Me, I do not understand it, either. I don't have the travel bug and all the bugs that come with it. But if I had a fiancée like his, I would move to Antarctica."

"And study tropical medicine there?" Giorgio asked dryly.

"It *is* very far south, George. Ah, poor Jack—he would rather get dysentery than be on the same continent as that awful Nadine."

Giorgio snorted but couldn't disagree. "Nothing is set in stone. Until I see them standing at the altar of that chapel on the family estate, I have to believe he may change his mind."

"But you won't!" Frank said gleefully. "Renata has caught you, line, sinker and hook. Bring her to meet me so I can see how the mighty have fallen."

Giorgio perked up his ears as several locks opened. They were in New York, after all, even if it was at a nice flat on the Upper West Side they'd chosen together.

Renata's family had been shocked to learn she was engaged, much less to a prince from a place they'd never even heard of. Her brothers had made him show them the official website of Vinciguerra before they believed it was a real country. He'd even had a hard time convincing them he wasn't a Eurotrash con man until he pulled up his online bio and official photo.

Her mother had quickly broken down into happy tears after that, and her grandmother had the unsettling habit of leering at him and then giving Renata a knowing wink.

Renata's Aunt Barbara and her friend Flick were going to run the bridal salon once Renata joined him full-time in Vinciguerra. She would design from a workshop in the palazzo and send them her creations. He couldn't wait for her to marry him and move there. His palazzo had all sorts of interesting nooks and crannies they could explore together. Naked.

"Giorgio, I'm home," the sweetest voice in the world called.

"Gotta go, Frank. Renata's back from work." He was already shutting down his laptop.

"Two's company, three's a crowd. I know when I'm not wanted—"

He laughed and hung up.

Renata appeared from the foyer, a sexy pout on her face—and a white box in her hands. "Look, Giorgio, my new shoes got wet. That stupid weather forecast never said anything about rain."

"I will buy you a thousand pairs if you come here and kiss me."

"Bribery, sex and shoes. I could get used to this." She sauntered over to him, purposely swaying her hips from side to side. Bright red toenails peeped out from the black high-heeled sandals. Today she wore one of his white dress shirts knotted at the waist over skintight dark denim capri pants. *Molto* sexy. She looked like a fifties starlet with one thing on her mind.

Lucky for him, he was of a like mind. "Come here."

"Wait a second, Giorgio." She shoved the white box at him. "This is for you."

He accepted it and lifted the lid. "What?" He inhaled the sweet fragrance in awe and pleasure. "No, these can't be." He picked up a delicate lemon cookie dusted in powdered sugar.

"Try it," she urged. "Stefania sent me your mother's recipe and my mom and grandma have been teaching me how to bake her cookies for you."

Giorgio was stunned. "You learned how to bake these—for me?"

"Of course. Don't just look at it, eat it."

He popped it into his mouth and springtime burst on his tongue, sunshine on a gloomy day. Just like Renata.

Yes, his mother's recipe, with a dash of Renata thrown in. How lucky a man he was to be loved by such women. His mother, his grandmother, his sister and now his fiancée. "I love you, Renata."

"And I love you, too." Renata puckered her lips into a luscious red pout. "Kiss me, so I know this is all real and not some crazy romantic comedy."

"Your wish is my command." He stood and pulled her into his arms.

She laughed and twined her arms around his neck. "Oh, Giorgio. I love you so much."

His heart flipped again, but this time it only made him smile instead of worry. He wordlessly scooped her up, wet shoes and all, and carried her off to bed where he proceeded to show her just how much he loved her, too.

* * * * *